AFTER THE FALL

EDITED BY
ROBERT SHECKLEY

SF
ace books
A Division of Charter Communications Inc.
A GROSSET & DUNLAP COMPANY
51 Madison Avenue
New York, New York 10010

AFTER THE FALL

Copyright © 1980 by Robert Sheckley

An ACE Book

First Ace Printing: September 1980

Printed Simultaneously in Canada

2 4 6 8 0 9 7 5 3 1

Manufactured in the United States of America

CONTENTS

AFTER THE FALL — Introduction

by
Robert Sheckley

Science fiction bears a certain resemblance to classical Greek drama in its use of variations on set themes. Drama in Periclean Athens dealt over and over again with the adventures of Hercules, Jason and Medea, Antigone, Agamemnon and Clytemnestra. In modern science fiction we have our own great themes: First Contact with Aliens, Invisibility, Time Travel, Parallel Worlds, to name a few. And, most venerable of all, we have The End of The World.

This perennially popular theme can be traced back to the Book of Revelations, and beyond. It is the great subject of the Norse sagas and the continual preoccupation of the Aztecs. It must be considered a universal archetype. Our own bookstores are crowded with fables of the coming destruction, most of them written in the heavy, portentous style suitable to so dire a theme.

For this anthology we have taken a variation on a variation. Our premise is that the end of the world might not be so bad after all. Although we will not go so far as to call it a laughing matter, still, it does seem that the destruction of ourselves and everything we hold dear could be considered with some levity, especially since we are only reading about it rather than undergoing it.

We could also point out that trying to get a laugh out of the end of the world is an act of faith in the indestructibility of our species. Nietzsche's Zarathustra (better known these days as the progenitor of Slan) said, "Let me have hobgoblins around me for I am courageous." To laugh at what you fear is the primordial human gesture, at least until something better comes along. That is the attitude we had in mind when we asked the authors in this collection to produce an 'upbeat end of the world story.'

But what is an upbeat end of the world story? We left the matter purposely vague, preferring to give the authors a chance to solve the situation for themselves, and also because we ourselves weren't entirely certain what an upbeat end of the world story would be like.

The results varied considerably, as you might imagine when different people write along the lines of an ambiguous directive. What we wanted to avoid at all costs was The Standard Downbeat End of the World Story. This type of story can be recognized by the following scene, which, in one form or another, invariably makes an appearance:

"Glak gazed out across the blackened landscape, noting the broken buildings jutting up from the scorched plain like decayed molars in the jaw of a demolished giant. The hellish scene was illuminated by the blue-green phosphorescence of deadly radioactivity, which, in combination with mutated germs, aerosol pollution and bubonic plague, had transformed the once verdant Earth into a charnel house. Glak smiled a sour radioactive smile as he considered all this, a dying man on a dying planet. Above him a blood-red moon watched sorrowfully as Glak scratched his initials in the debris, the last meaningless message of the final sentient creature on the dead sphere that whirled heedlessly through the sterile heavens. And then, just as his eyes were beginning to dim, Glak made out vast dark shapes dropping down out of the night sky and carrying enormous vacuum cleaners and dustbins. And then Glak understood that the drama of humanity was over, and that all of human history, Alexander and Rome, Paris and the Empire State Building, Roller Derby, sausages, everything human, had been reduced to a few electrochemical interchanges in the dying brain of the last man. How tacky, Glak thought. And then he was dead, and mankind was dead, and all animal, vegetable and insect life was dead, and the howling wind whirled an empty Campbell's soup can around the clumsy uncomprehending feet of the robotic aliens . . ."

We have no stories like that in this collection. Our authors have taken many different approaches to The Event. Phil Farmer sees it as a spectacle to be filmed by Cecil B. DeMille, with script by Harlan Ellison, and with God as the producer. Bob Shaw's end of the world starts with a con job, and Bill Nolan's detective Sam Space finds himself involved in a larger case than he had imagined. Maxim Jabukowski takes us through The End that every science fiction writer is waiting for: the destruction of everyone except a small elite of s-f writers and their ladies. Ian Watson takes a very positive approach to Termination, producing a sexual apocalypse that just might be worth dying for. Roger Zelazny gives us three haunting closeups of the time of destruction. Harry Harrison's tale of the last two survivors of Earth, one man and one woman, proves what we have long suspected: that for some women the motive of revenge is intimately connected with the procreative drive. J. A. Lawrence shows elegiacally that the end of the world is not necessarily bad news for everyone. And Thomas Disch's eschatological study presents hitherto unsuspected insights into the Italian confection known as the *canolle*, employing it to good effect in the figure of speech called, in classic rhetoric, *oxymoron*, or mating of incongruities. I myself have written a story for this collection, but modesty forbids me to say anything about it except that it is short.

I am especially pleased to present three authors making their debut in science fiction. Simon Gandolfi, a former soldier of fortune who served in the First Zulu War tells me that he had to punch out three typewriters before one of them would cough up the story he was after. Joel Schulman, a Canadian edelweiss manufacturer, took time out from his hobby of turning wooden ducks on a lathe to present his powerful and evocative story. And K. Copeland Shea wrote her story while correcting proofs for her new book on her experiences as Albert Schweitzer's unacknowledged mistress, to be published later this year by Underground Comix.

This is my first anthology, and I dedicate it in all sincerity and gratitude to Abby, without whose valuable work of harassing lazy authors (including yours truly) and getting this thing together while I was travelling in Asia researching noodles this book would have remained no more than a glimmer in Jim Baen's crazed mind.

END

THE LAST DAYS OF (PARALLEL?) EARTH

by
Robert Sheckley

When the end of the world was announced, Rachel and I decided not to break up after all. "What would be the sense?" Rachel asked me. "We will have no time to form other relationships." I nodded, but I was not convinced. I was worried about what would happen if the world did not end, if the great event was delayed, postponed, held over indefinitely. There might have been a miscalculation concerning the effect of the Z Field, the scientists might have been wrong about the meaning of the Saperstein Conjunction, and there we would be, Rachel and I with our eternal complaints, and our children with their eternal complaints, bound together by apocalyptic conjunction stronger than our marriage vows, for eternity or until Armageddon, whichever came first. I put this to Rachel in what I hoped was a nice way, and she said to me, "Don't worry, if the world does not end on schedule as predicted by eminent scientists you will return to

your dismal furnished apartment and I will stay
here with the children and my lover."

That was reassuring of her, and of course I
didn't want to spend the end of the world by
myself in the dismal furnished apartment I
shared with the Japanese girl and her English
boyfriend and no television. There would be
nothing to do there but listen to the Japanese girl
talk to her friends on the telephone and eat in
the Chinese restaurant which had promised to
stay open throughout the end of the world or as
long as physically possible, since the owner did
not believe in making changes hastily.

You said, "I don't want to face anything like
this straight," so you brought out your entire
stash, the Thai sticks, the speckled brown co-
caine, the acid in the form of tiny red stars, the
gnarled mushrooms from god knows where, the
red Lebanese and the green Moroccan, yes, and
your last few treasured Quaaludes, and a few
Mogadon for good measure. You said, "Let's pool
our mind-blowing resources and go out before
we come down."

Other people had made their own preparations.
The airlines were running end-of-the-world specials to Ultima Thule, Valparaiso, Kuala Lumpur;
kinky trips for demising people. The networks
were making a lot of the event, of course. Some
of our favorite programs were cut, replaced by
End of the World Specials. We tuned into The
Last Talkathon on CBS: "Well, gosh, folks, it sure
looks like the kite is going up at last. I have a
guest here, Professor Mandrax from UCLA, who
is going to explain to us just how the big snuff
is going to come about."

Whatever channel you turned to, there were physicists, mathematicians, biologists, chemists, linguistic philosophers, and commentators to try to explain what they were explaining. Professor Johnson the eminent cosmologist, said, "Well, of course, it's not exactly a cosmological event, except metaphorically, in its effect upon us. We humans, in our parochial way, consider these things to be very important. But I can assure you that on the scale of magnitude I work on, this event is of no significance, is banal, in fact, our little O type sun entering the Z field just at the time of the Saperstein Conjunction, with the ensuing disarrangement of local conditions. I am imprecise on purpose, of course, since Indeterminacy renders exactitude a 19th century hangup. But Professor Weaver of the Philosophy Department might have more to say about that."

"Well, yes," Professor Weaver said, " 'end of the world' is somewhat of a loose expression. What we are faced with is a viewpoint problem. We could say that, from some other point of observation, if such exists, this ending is the end of nothing at all. Just one moment of pain, my dear, and then eternal life, to quote The Poet."

On another channel we heard that the Army was issuing turkey dinners to all our servicemen in Germany, and their families, of course. There had been some talk of flying them all home, but we decided to keep them in position in case it was not the end of the world after all but instead some devious communistic scheme such as we know the Russians are capable of with their twisted sense of humor and their implacable will to give everyone a hard time. And we heard that

the Chinese hadn't even announced the fact, or
so-called fact, to their population at large, except
obliquely, in the form of posters no larger than
postage stamps, signed by 'A Concerned Neighbor from Neighborhood C.'

And you couldn't understand why Edward,
your lover, insisted upon staying in his room and
working on his novel. "It's not *apropos* any
longer," you told him. "There's not going to be
anyone around to publish it or read it." "What
has that got to do with it?" Edward asked, and
winked at me. I understood perfectly, was in fact
working like a berserker to finish my own account
of the last day, yes, and with great pleasure, for
the end of the world presents a writer with the
greatest deadline of them all, the ultimate deadline: twelve o'clock midnight tonight and that's
all she wrote, folks. What a challenge! I knew
that artists all over the world were responding
to it, that an end-of-the-world *ouevre* was being
created that might be of interest to historians in
a world parallel to our own in which this catastrophe did not take place.

"Well, yes," Professor Carpenter said, "the
concept of parallel universes is I would say licit,
but unprovable, at least in the time we have left.
I myself would consider it a wish fulfillment fantasy, though my good friend Professor Mung, the
eminent psychologist, is more competent to
speak of that than I."

You made your famous turkey dinner that
night, with the stuffing and the cranberry sauce
and the sweet potato pie with meringue topping,
and you even made your special Chinese spare-
ribs as an extra treat, even though the Chinese

refused to believe in the event except in postage-stamp-size posters of oriental foreboding. And everyone in the world began smoking cigarettes again, except for the irreducible few who did not believe in the end of the world and were therefore still scared of lung cancer. And people on their death beds struggled to stay alive a little longer, just a little longer, so that when I go, the whole damn thing goes. And some doctors stayed on call, declaring it their ludicrous duty, while others compulsively played golf and tennis and tried to forget about improving their strokes.

The turkey with four drumsticks and eight wings. Lewd displays on television: since all is over, all is allowed. The compulsive answering of business letters: Dear Joe, take your contract and stick it up your giggie the show is over and I can finally tell you what a crap artist you are, but if there is any mistake about The End I want you to know that this letter is meant as a joke which I'm sure that you as the very special person you are can appreciate.

All of us were caught between the irreconcilable demands of abandonment and caution. What if we are not to die? Even belief in the end of the world required an act of faith on the part of dishwashers as well as university professors.

And that last night of creation I gave up cigarettes forever. An absurdity. What difference did it make? I did it because you had always told me that absurdities made a difference, and I had always known that, so I threw away my pack of Marlboro and listened while Professor Mung said, "Wish fulfillment, or its obverse, Death Wish Fulfillment, cannot licitly be generalized

into an objective correlative, to use Elliott's term.
But if we take Jung into our synthesis, and consider this ending as an archetype, not to say *Weltanschauung*, our understanding increases as our *tiempo para gastarlo* disappears into the black hole of the past which contains all our hopes and endeavors."

The final hour came at last. I carved the turkey and Edward came out of his room long enough to take a plateful of breast and ask for my comments on his final rewrite of his last chapter, and I said, "It still needs work," and you said, "That's cruel," and Edward said, "Yes, I thought it needed something myself," and went back to his room. Outside the streets were deserted except for the unfortunate few who couldn't get to a television set, and we did up all the remaining drugs and switched wildly between channels. I had brought my typewriter into the kitchen and I was getting it all down, and you talked of the holidays we should have taken, and I thought about the women I should have loved, and at five to twelve Edward came out of his room again and showed me the re-rewritten last chapter, and I said, "You've got it this time," and he said, "I thought so, is there any more coke left?" And we did up the rest of the drugs and you said to me, "For Chrissakes, can't you stop typing?" And I said, "I have to get it all down," and you hugged me, and Edward hugged me, and the three of us hugged the children whom we had allowed to stay up late because it was the end of the world, and I said to you, "Look, I'm sorry about everything," and you said, "I'm sorry, too," and Edward said, "I don't think I did anything wrong, but I'm sorry, too." "Sorry about what?" the children asked, but before we had a chance to tell them, before we could even decide what we were sorry about,

THE DAY AFTER THE END OF THE WORLD
by
Harry Harrison

It wasn't a very big piece of the world, but it was all that was left. Around it in space floated other fragments of the destroyed planet, just chunks of rock and dirt and bits of debris. But the large piece had the best part of a farmhouse on it, with a tree in front, and a patch of grass with a frozen sheep standing on it. The sheep was staring in a very fixed manner. That was all there was. The sheer edge dropped away on all sides, just bare dirt with bits of root sticking out of it. The man sat on the edge of the world, his legs dangling, and dropped a twig over. It fell swiftly from sight. His name was Frank and the girl, in the swing hanging from the branch of the tree, was named Gwen.

"It's not like I tried to force you or anything," Frank said, looking very glum. "You know, or be beastly. I was just upset, you should understand that, what with the end of the world and everything. Feeling very lonely. I thought maybe, you know, a little kiss would help me forget. Help us both forget."

"Yes, Frank," Gwenn said and pushed with her foot so she swung a bit.

"So you really had no cause to slap me. We are shipmates after all."

"I said that I was sorry I hit you, Frank. I'm a little upset too, you should understand that. It's not every day that this sort of thing happens."

"No, not every day."

"You shouldn't be angry at me. Can you give me a push?"

"It's not that I'm angry," he said, standing and brushing the bits of frozen grass from the leg of his uniform. "Hurt maybe, depressed really. Struck by the woman I love." He gave the swing an indifferent shove.

"Please don't start that talk again, Frank. It's all over. You just say that because you want to do you-know-what with me. And you know I love someone else."

"Gwenn darling, face facts. You're not going to see Robert again, ever . . ."

"You can't be sure."

"Believe me, I'm sure. The whole world's blown up, bang, just like that, without warning, and everyone with it. We were in the spaceship on the other side of the moon or we would have blown up too. But Robert's gone with it. He was in Minneapolis and Minneapolis is gone."

"We don't know."

"We know. I don't think Minneapolis had any special dispensation. All we found with the search radar is this chunk of the world. This is the biggest piece that there is."

Gwenn frowned at the thought and put out her leg so the swing stopped. "There might be a piece of Minneapolis too . . . "

"And if Robert is on it he is frozen just like that sheep."

"You're so cruel — you just want to hurt me!"

"No, please." He took her by the shoulders carefully, standing behind her. "I want anything but that. It's just that you must face up to the truth. There's just you and me now. And I love you. I mean that, sincerely."

While he spoke his hands gently caressed her shoulders and moved down her arms, out onto the sweet swell of her breasts. But Gwenn shrugged out of his embrace and jumped to her feet, walking quickly away from him. She looked down at the immobile sheep.

"I wonder if he felt anything," she asked.

"Who — Robert or the sheep?"

"Ohh, you *are* cruel!"

She stamped her foot in anger — then raised her hand as he moved towards her. Frank growled something indecipherable under his breath and dropped into the swing.

"Let's be realistic," he said. "Let's forget everything that happened on the ship. Forget I made a pass at you, forget that I tried to get you into the sack. Forget it. Let's start fresh. Face the situation that we're in. The two of us alone. I'm Adam and you're Eve . . ."

"Gwenn."

"I *know* your name is Gwenn. I mean we're like Adam and Eve and it is up to us to keep the human race going. Do you understand?"

"Yes. You're still trying to seduce me."

"God damn it, it doesn't matter what you think! It's our duty. We may have been spared by divine providence . . ."

"You told me that you were an atheist."

"Well you said that you go to church. I'm looking at it from your point of view."

"And I'm looking at it from yours. You're oversexed."

"Be happy that I am. We must be fruitful. We owe it to the human race."

Gwenn patted the sheep's head, deep in thought. "I don't know," she finally said. "It might be best to end it all right here. We blew up the world, didn't we? That's what you might call pollution on a really impressive scale."

"You can't mean that. We don't know what happened. It could have been an accident . . ."

"Some accident!"

"Well, you know . . ." Frank jumped from the swing and came towards her. "Forget the human race then," he pleaded. "Think of you and I. The two of us. The warmth of contact, the end of loneliness, the thrill of the kiss, touch of flesh . . ."

"If you come any closer I'll scream!"

"Scream away!" Frank shouted, angry and bitter, grabbing her, pulling her to him. "Who's going to hear? I love you . . . want you . . . need you . . ."

She pushed at him desperately, turning her face back and forth away from his but he was far stronger. He kissed her neck, her cheek — and she stopped struggling.

"Are you some kind of rapist?" she asked in a very low voice, looking him straight in the eyes.

For a moment longer he held her. Then dropped his hands and stepped away.

"No. I'm not a rapist. Just a nice middle-class boy with a strong sex drive and plenty of guilt."

"That's better."

"It is not better — it's a lot worse! I mean what am I doing, the last man alive on Earth, feeling guilt? My bourgeois world is gone but I still carry it around with me. What do you think would happen to you if I were a real male chauvinist pig and just grabbed you and worked my will upon you?"

"Don't talk dirty."

"I'm not talking dirty — I'm just trying to knock some sense through your dumb blonde head. It's you and I, get it? Just the two of us. We've got this chunk of the world and I've anchored our spaceship under it to give us gravity and air and the atomic pile will keep it this way for a thousand years. The food synthesizer will make all the food we need so we are all set, in a manner of speaking."

"All set for what?"

"That's what I'm asking you. Are we going to grow old gracefully, and separately, just good chums, you knitting and me watching old TV tapes? Do you want that?"

"I didn't think much of that dumb blond remark."

"Don't change the subject. Is that the way you want it?"

"I haven't thought about it . . ."

"Well think. We're here. Alone. For the rest of our lives."

"It does bear thinking about." She cocked her

head to the side and looked at him, as though for the first time. "You can kiss me if you like," she said.

"That's more like it!"

"But no funny business. Just that. In the nature of an experiment you might say."

Now invited, Frank approached almost shyly. Gwenn had her eyes closed and she shivered when he put his arms around her. He drew her close, held her to him, lowered his lips and kissed her closed eyes. She trembled again but did not move away. Nor did she protest when his lips found her mouth, kissing long and lovingly. When he dropped his arms and stepped back she slowly opened her eyes; he smiled at her tenderly.

"Robert kissed better," she said.

In a sudden rage Frank kicked the sheep —then hopped around holding his foot and moaning in pain for the solidly frozen sheep was hard as rock.

"And I suppose he was good in bed too," he said bitterly.

"He was marvellous," Gwenn admitted. "Just wonderful. That's why I find it so hard to even look at another man. And I'm carrying his baby and that makes it even more difficult."

"You are what . . .?"

"Pregnant. These things happen, you know. Robert doesn't know yet . . ."

"Nor will he ever."

"Don't be horrid."

"Sorry. This is wonderful, greatest news ever. We've just increased the gene pool of the human race by fifty percent. Robert's son can marry our daughter, or vice versa."

"That's incest!"

"It wasn't incest in the Bible, was it? Not when you are starting the world, that's the rule. It's only incest much later on."

Gwenn walked over and sat in the swing again, thinking deeply. Then she sighed.

"It just won't work," she said. "It goes against everything. First you want us to make love without being married, and that's a sin . . ."

"You did it with Robert!"

"Yes, but we planned to get married some day. But now we can't. Nor can you and I be married because there is no one to marry us. And you want to have children and have them commit incest — it's just too horrible. That's no way to start a world."

"Do you have any better ideas?"

"No, not really. But I don't like yours."

Frank dropped heavily to the ground and shook his head with astonishment.

"I just can't believe this is happening," he said, mostly to himself. "The last man alive and the last woman alive and we're arguing theology." He sprang to his feet in sudden anger.

"No! I'm not going to argue any more, nor discuss it." He tore at his shirt, struggling to take it off. "It all begins again, right here, now. The world starts afresh. I will not be lumbered by a moral code that is just as disintegrated as the planet that bore it. I am all. The language I speak will be the language of all the generations to come. If I say ugggh for water everyone, forever, will say ugh and never question it. My power is godlike!"

"You're crazy!" She drew away as he advanced.

"I am if I want to be. I am all. I shall ravish you and beat you and you will love me for it. If you don't I'll beat you some more. Now why don't you scream?" He threw his shirt to the ground and advanced on her. "I'm the only one who will hear the scream and I don't care about it."

He undid his fly and she uttered a muffled scream. He only laughed.

"Make the choice!" he shouted. "Enjoy it or hate it for it makes no difference to me. I am godhead, spermbearer, almighty. From my loins a new race will spring . . ."

He stopped suddenly as they both swayed.

"Did you feel that?" Frank asked. Gwenn nodded. "The ground, it moved as though something bumped into us."

"Another ship!" he said, quickly closing his fly. He grabbed up his shirt and hurried to put it on. Gwenn pushed her hair with her hand and wished that she had a mirror with her.

"There's someone coming," Frank said, pointing, "there."

They drew together unconsciously at the scratching from below their world. There was the sound of panting breath and a man climbed painfully up over the edge. He wore a one-piece boiler suit with only his head and hands exposed.

They were green.

"He's . . . green," Gwenn said. Frank did not have a ready answer. The man climbed to his feet and brushed dirt from his hands and bowed slightly in their direction.

"I hope I'm not intruding," he said.

"No, that's fine," Gwenn said. "Do come in."

"Why are you green?" Frank asked.

"I might very well ask why you are pink."

"No jokes," Frank shouted, making a fist. "Or else . . ."

"I'm very sorry," the man said, raising his green hands and taking a step backwards. "I do beg your pardon. All of this is very upsetting, as it must be to you. I am green because I am not human. I am from another world."

"A little green man!" Gwenn gasped.

"I'm not that little," the man pouted.

"I'm Frank and this is Gwenn."

"Pleased to meet you, I'm sure. You would find my name hard to pronounce so I suggest that you call me Robert."

"Not, Robert!" Gwenn wailed. "He's dead."

"I do beg your pardon. Anything then. Would Horace suit?"

"Horace, just what are you doing here?" Frank asked.

"Well, now that's a little complicated. If I might begin at the beginning . . ."

"How is it you speak English so well?" Gwenn said.

"That comes later too, if you will bear with me." He strolled back and forth, marking his points on his fingers. "Firstly, I come from a distant planet around a sun a good number of parsecs from here. We're doing a survey and I was assigned this section of the galaxy. When I first saw your world I was most impressed. Green, as you can well imagine, is a favourite colour of ours. I set the recorders rolling and made as complete a record as I could in a limited time. That would be a bit over two hundred of your years."

"You don't look that old," Gwenn said.

"Different lifespans, you know. I won't tempt your credulity by giving my real age."

"I'm twenty-two," she said.

"How very nice. Now, if I might continue. I recorded everything as I have been trained to do, learned a few of your languages — I do pride myself on a certain linguistic ability — and bit by bit I came to a singularly horrifying realization. The human race is, was I should say, a rather nasty piece of work."

"You're not much of a charmer yourself either, greeny," Frank called out. Horace chose to ignore the outburst.

"By that I mean to say yours is a most successful race, strong, intelligent, fertile, most successful indeed. It was the way that you obtained that success that was so frightening. You are killers."

"Survival," Frank said firmly. "We had no other choice. Eat or be eaten, kill or be killed. Survival of the fittest."

"I'll not argue with that. There is of course only one way for any race to survive and I appreciate the point. It's what a race does after it has taken over a world that interests me. Ours became the dominant race on our planet many eons ago. Since then we have preserved the other species. The rule of peace and law has prevailed. While your people, while wiping out the other species, were still not satisfied and continued to kill one another as well. I found it most depressing."

"No one asked your opinion," Frank said.

"Of course. But I still know what I observed

and it not only depressed me, but made me worried as well. My planet is not that distant, astronomically speaking, and it was within reason that you might find us one day. And if you did you would probably try to kill us as well."

"I don't think there is much chance of that now," Gwenn said, dropping into the swing and looking unhappy once again.

"Yes, it may be a theoretical point now, but it must be considered nevertheless. So there was I, an intelligent and peaceful individual, a vegetarian who would never consider harming as much as a fly, there was I worrying about the possible destruction of my world. It was a moral dilemma as you can see."

"No I can't," Frank said, shaking his head. Then he snapped his head up. "Say — did you have anything to do with what happened to the world?"

"I'll get to that in a moment."

"A simple yes or no now will do."

"Nothing is ever that simple. Please hear me out. It was most dramatic you see, for there I was firmly mounted on the horns of this dilemma. And no one to help me decide. The voyage home is quite a long one and by the time I would have made it and consulted with my superiors and they had made their minds up, well you people might very well have made your own starships and have been on the way to visit us. No, I had to make my mind up right there and then. If I did nothing you would build your ships and come and destroy us. There I was, a creature of peace, thinking the unthinkable."

"You *did* blow up the world!" Frank said,

striding forward.

"Please! No violence!" Horace said, raising his hands and shying away. "I can't stand violence." Frank stopped, wanting to hear the rest, yet his fists were still clenched. "Thank you, Frank. As I was saying I was thinking the unthinkable. I could not resort to violence to make peace — or could I? If I did nothing my people would be destroyed. So it came down to a choice between which race was to survive. Yours or mine. So of course when it was phrased that way the answer was clear. Mine. Since we are far older and more intelligent, generally more interesting and attractive than you are. And peaceful."

"So you blew up our world," Frank said in a low voice.

"That wasn't very peaceful," Gwenn said.

"No, I suppose that it wasn't. But it was just an isolated case, really. After a great many centuries of peace in the past, and of course many more to come in the future."

"Why are you here?" Frank asked. "Why are you telling us this?"

"Why — to apologise of course. I'm very sorry it had to work out like this."

"Not half as sorry as we are, you bright green son of a bitch."

"Well if I thought you weren't going to be gentlemanly about it I wouldn't have come."

Frank lunged forward, but Gwenn came between them, stopping him.

"Frank, please," she begged. "I can't bear the thought of any more violence. I shall scream. And you did this all by yourself, Mr. Horace?"

"Horace, a forename, if you please. Yes I did.

I take all of the responsibility."

"What about the others aboard your ship?" she asked.

"I am alone. Very automated you know. It took me awhile to work out the formula, I don't think there has ever been a planet-buster bomb before, but I did it in the end. It wasn't easy, but I did it. For the sake of peace."

"That has a familiar ring to it," Frank said.

"I am quoting one of your generals in a war a few years ago. 'I killed them in order to save them.' But I'm not that hypocritical. I killed your planet in order to save mine. Just playing by your rules, you see."

"I see," Frank said, very calmly. "But you said you were alone. How about the other green man climbing over the ledge, there behind you?"

"Impossible, I assure you."

When he turned to look, Frank stepped forward and struck him a mighty blow on the jaw. The alien folded nicely and Frank sat on him and choked him until the body was still. Gwenn looked on and nodded approvingly.

"I'll take the feet," Frank said.

Without another word they carried the body to the edge of the cliff and slung it over, watching as it spiraled out among the rest of the space debris.

"We have to find his ship," Frank said.

"No, kiss me first. Hard."

"Yum," Frank said long moments later when he emerged from the embrace breathless and happy. "That was pretty good. Might I ask what brought it on?"

"I want to get used to your kisses, your embraces. We will have to raise a large family if we intend to repopulate the entire world."

"I couldn't agree more. Could I also ask you what made you change your mind?"

"Him. That creature. He can't get away with it."

"You're damn right! Revenge! Raise the family, teach them to fly, build bombs, go out and find those alien bastards and blow them out of space. Prove that he was right after all. We'll get our revenge."

"I certainly hope so. He can't kill my Robert and get away with it."

"Robert! Is that why you're doing this? What about everyone else, the billions, the rest of the world?"

"I didn't know anyone else in Minneapolis."

"If Horace had known about Robert I'll bet you he would have thought twice about blowing up the world."

"Well he didn't and that was his mistake. Shall we go now?"

"Do you want to bring the sheep?"

Gwenn looked at it and frowned in thought, "No," she finally said. "It looks so nice there. And it will give us something to come home to."

"Right. Out for revenge. Make plans. Build bombs, raise children for vengeance. Destroy."

"It doesn't sound so nice when you say it that way."

Frank rubbed his jaw. "Now that you mention it, it doesn't. But we really have no choice."

"Don't we? Just because that horrible little green man blew up a whole world, it doesn't mean that we have to act the same way."

"Of course it doesn't. But there is justice! An eye for an eye, you know the sort of thing."

"I do. I am well read in the Old Testament. But just because this was done and we learned to do it, that doesn't mean that it's right, does it?"

"I find your syntax difficult but your thought simple. What you are trying to say is that our world is gone. We can't restore it by blowing up another world. If the aliens are as peaceful as Horace said, then it would be a crime to destroy them as well. After all — they didn't blow up the world."

"It makes you pause to think."

"It sure does — and I'm sorry that I did. There was something nice and clearcut about blowing up their planet because they blew up ours."

"I know. But still, it's a bad habit to get into."

"You're right. Start blowing up planets and you never know where it will end. So we have a chance not to go on with the old eye-for-eye tooth-for-tooth business. If we build our own world, just you and I and our kids, we'll be building on something other than vengeance for a change. That's a big challenge."

Gwenn dropped heavily into the swing. "I get a little frightened when you talk like that," she said. "It's a big enough responsibility starting a whole world, but starting a whole moral system is even more important. No killing, no violence . . ."

"Peace and love on earth to all men. The sort of thing the church was saying while they were blessing the troops. Only this time we would mean it. Turn the other cheek in a really big way. Forget the fact that they blew up our world. Prove that Horace was wrong. Then, when we meet them some day, they would have to apologise for him."

"We apologise for him right now," the green man said, climbing up over the edge of the world.

Gwenn screamed and fell back. "Horace — you're not dead!" she gasped.

The green man shook his head. "Sorry," he said, "but the individual you knew as Horace is dead. And after what I have heard just now I tend to agree that his death was richly deserved. He destroyed a world and was punished for it."

"Horace said that he was alone," Frank said; his fists were clenched again.

"He lied. There were two of us and he volunteered to meet with you two, the only survivors and explain what had happened. I will bring the recording back to our planet. There will be great mourning at the destruction of your world."

"Thanks," Frank said, in a very unthankful voice. "It really makes me feel better. And you helped him blow up the world?"

The green man thought for a moment, then nodded reluctantly.

"Help is too strong a word. In the beginning I disagreed with his analysis of the situation. In the end I reluctantly agreed . . ."

"You helped. So now you go home and tell everyone what happened, and tell them that the survivors are building a new world and maybe you had better think of blowing us up too in case our descendants aren't as generous and understanding as we are. They might want to come and blow you up as a precautionary measure."

"No, really, I wouldn't advise a course of action like that . . ."

"But there is a possibility that it might be done in any case, despite your advice?"

"I hope not. But there is of course always the

possibility . . ."

"Another green son-of-a-bitch," Gwenn said, drawing a small pistol from her pocket and shooting the alien.

"That about sums it up," Frank said, sighing, looking at the crumpled body. "I suppose now we'll have to find their ship and kill any more of them that might be there."

"And then take the ship and go blow their planet up," Gwenn added.

"No other choice. As Horace said, we have a reputation for this sort of thing. Best to live up to it."

"I wouldn't be comfortable if we didn't," Gwenn said. "I would worry about our children and their children, you know. Best to get it over with."

"You're right of course. And after we blow them up then we'll teach the kids about turning the other cheek and that kind of thing. It will be all right then."

"Shall we go now?"

"I guess we had better," Gwenn said, looking around at the last little bit of the world. "It may be a long trip so the earlier we start the better. Do we want to bring the sheep?"

"No, I'll turn the air off. It will keep nicely. It looks so peaceful here. And it will give us something to come home to."

A VERY GOOD YEAR...
by
Roger Zelazny

"Hello," he said.

She looked at him. He was sandy-haired, thirtyish, a little rugged-looking but well-groomed and very well-dressed. He was smiling.

"I'm sorry," she said. "Do I know you?"

He shook his head.

"Not yet," he said. "Bradley's the name. Brad Dent."

"Well . . . What can I do for you, Mr. Dent?"

"I believe that I am going to fall in love with you," he said. "Of course, this requires a little cooperation. May I ask what time you get off work?"

"You're serious!"

"Yes."

She looked down at the countertop, noticed that her fingers were tapping the glass, stilled them, looked back up. His smile was still there.

"We close in twenty minutes," she said abruptly. "I could be out front in half an hour."

"Will you?"

She smiled then. She nodded.

"My name's Marcia."

"I'm glad," he said.

At dinner, in a restaurant she would never have found by herself, she studied him through the candlelight. His hands were smooth. His accent was Middle American.

"You looked familiar when you came up to me," she said. "I've seen you around somewhere before. In fact, now that I think back on it, I believe you passed my counter several times today."

"Probably," he said, filling her wine glass.

"What do you do, Brad?"

"Nothing," he said.

She laughed.

"Doesn't sound very interesting."

He smiled again.

"What I mean to say is that I am devoting myself to enjoying this year, not working."

"Why is that?"

"I can afford it, and it's a very good year."

"In what ways is it special?"

He leaned back, laced his fingers, looked at her across them.

"There are no wars going on anywhere, for a change," he finally said. "No civil unrest either. The economy is wonderfully stable. The weather is beautiful." He raised his glass and took a sip. "There are some truly excellent vintages available. All of my favorite shows and movies are playing. Science is doing exciting things — in medicine, in space. A flock of fine books has been published. There are so many places to go, things to do this year. It could take a lifetime." He reached out and touched her hand. "And I'm in love," he finished.

She blushed.

"You hardly know me . . ."

". . . And I have that to look forward to, also — getting to know you."

"You *are* very strange," she said.

"But you will see me again . . ."

"If it's going to be that kind of year," she said, and she squeezed his hand.

She saw him regularly for a month before she quit her job and moved in with him. They dined well, they traveled often . . .

She realized, one evening in Maui near the end of the year, that she was in love with him.

"Brad," she said, clasping him tightly, "this spring it seemed more like a game than anything else . . ."

"And now?"

"Now it's special."

"I'm glad."

On New Year's Eve, they went to dinner at a place he knew in Chinatown. She leaned forward over the Chicken Fried Rice.

"That man," she said, "at the corner table, to the right . . ."

"Yes?"

"He looks a lot like you."

Brad glanced over, nodded.

"Yes."

"You know, I still don't know you very well."

"But we know each other better."

"Yes, that's true. But — Brad, that man coming out of the rest room . . ."

He turned his head.

"He looks like you, too."

"He does."

"Strange . . . I mean, I don't even know where you get your money."

"My family," he said, "always had a lot."

She nodded.

"I see. — Two more! Those men who just came in!'

"Yes, they look like me, too."

She shook her head.

"Then you really never had to work?"

"On the contrary. I'm a scientist. Bet I could have had the Nobel Prize."

She dished out some Sweet and Sour Pork. Then she paused, eyes wide, head turned again.

"Brad, it *has* to be more than coincidence. There's *another* you!"

"Yes," he said, "I always dine here on New Year's Eve."

She lay down her fork. She paled.

"You're a biologist," she said, "aren't you? And you've cloned yourself? Maybe you're not even the original . . ."

He laughed softly.

"No, I'm a physicist," he said, "and I'm not a clone. It *has* been a very good year, hasn't it?"

She smiled gently. She nodded.

"Of course it has," she said. "You say you *always* dine here on New Year's Eve?"

"Yes. The same New Year's Eve. This one."

"Time travel?"

"Yes."

"Why?"

"This has been such a good year that I have

resolved to live it over, and over and over — for the rest of my life."

Two couples entered the restaurant. She looked back.

"That's us!" she said. "And the second couple looks a lot older — but they're us, too!"

"Yes, this is where I first saw you. I had to find you after that. We looked so happy."

"Why have we never met any of them before?"

"I keep a diary. We'll go to different places each time around. Except for New Year's Eve . . ."

She raked her lower lip once with her teeth.

"Why — Why keep repeating it?" she finally asked.

"It's been such a very good year," he said.

"But what comes after?"

He shrugged.

"Don't ask me."

He turned and smiled at the older couple, who had nodded toward them.

"I think they're coming over. Perhaps we can buy them a drink. Isn't she lovely?"

FIRE AND/OR ICE
by
Roger Zelazny

"Mommy! Mommy!"

"Yes?"

"Yes?"

"Tell me again what you did in the war."

"Nothing much. Go play with your sisters."

"I've been doing that all afternoon. They play too hard. I want to hear about the bad winter and the monsters and all."

"That's what it was, a bad winter."

"How cold was it, Mommy?"

"It was so cold that brass monkeys were singing soprano on every corner. It was so cold that it lasted for three years and the sun and the moon grew pale, and sister killed sister and daughters knocked off mommies for a Zippo lighter and a handful of pencil shavings."

"Then what happened?"

"Another winter came along, of course. A lot worse than the first."

"How bad was it?"

"Well, the two giant wolves who had been chasing the sun and the moon across the sky finally caught them and ate them. Damned dark then, but the blood that kept raining down gave a little light to watch the earthquakes and hurricanes by, when you could see through the blizzards.''

"How come we don't have winters like that anymore?''

"Used them all up for awhile, I suppose.''

"How come there's a sun up in the sky now, if it got eaten?''

"Oh, that's the new one. It didn't happen till after the fires and the boiling oceans and all.''

"Were you scared?''

"What scared me was what came later, when a giant snake crawled out of the sea and started fighting with this big person with the hammer. Then gangs of giants and monsters came from all directions and got to fighting with each other. And then there was a big, old, one-eyed person with a spear, stabbing away at a giant wolf which finally ate him, beard and all. Then another person came along and killed the wolf. All of a sudden, it looked familiar and I went outside and caught one of the troops by the sleeve.

" 'Hey, this is Götterdämmerung,' I said, 'isn't it?'

"A nearby tv crew moved in on us as the person paused in hacking away at an amorphous mass with lots of eyes and nodded.

" 'Sure is,' he said. 'Say, you must be —' and then the amorphous mass ate him.

"I crossed the street to where another one in a horned helmet was performing atrocities on a fallen foeperson.

" 'Pardon me,' I asked him, 'but who are you?'

" 'Loki's the name,' was the reply. 'What is your part in all of this?'

" 'I don't know that I have a part,' I said. 'But that other person started to say something like I might and then the amorphous mass which was just stepped on by the giant with the arrow in his throat sucked him in.'

"Loki dispatched his victim with a look of regret and studied my torn garment.

" 'You're dressed like a man,' he said, 'but — '

"I drew my shirt together.

" 'I am —' I began.

" 'Sure. Here's a safety pin. What a fine idea you've just given me! Come this way.

" 'There've got to be two human survivors,' he explained, pushing a path through a pack of werewolves. 'The gods will give their lives to defend you, once I've delivered you to Hodd-mimir's Holt — that's the designated fallout shelter.' He snatched up an unconscious woman and slung her over his shoulder. 'You'll live through all this. A new day will dawn, a glorious new world will be revealed requiring a new first couple. Seeing you waiting, the gods will die believing that all is well —' He broke into a fit of laughter. 'They think that all the deaths will bring a new regime, of love, peace and happiness — and a new race . . .' The tears streamed down his face. 'All tragedies require liberal doses of irony,' he concluded, as he bore us in a psychedelic chariot through rivers of blood and fields of bones.

"He deposited us here, amid warmth, trees,

fountains, singing birds — all those little things
that make life pleasant and trite: plenty of food,
gentle breezes, an attractive house with indoor
plumbing. Then, still laughing, he returned to the
front.

"Later, my companion awoke — blonde and
lithe and lovely — and her eyes flashed when she
turned my way.

" 'So,' she snapped, 'you drag me from this
horrible masculine conflict that I may serve your
lusts in a secret pleasure haven! I'll have none
of it, after all you've done to me!'

"I moved to comfort her, but she dropped into
a karate stance.

" 'Tell me,' I said then, 'what you mean. Nothing has been done to you —'

" 'You call leaving a girl pregnant nothing?'
she cried. 'With all the abortionists busy treating
frostbite? No! I want no part of men, never again!'

" 'Be of good cheer, sister,' I replied, unpinning
my shirt. 'I found myself too attractive to men,
not to mention weak-willed — this long night
being what it is — and suffering with a similar
medical quandary, I resolved in a fit of remorse
to lead the life of a simple transvestite.'

" 'Sappho be praised!' she replied.

"And we both had twins, and lived happily
ever after. Winter faded, and the Twilight of the
Gods passed. The world is a new place, of love,
peace and happiness, for so long as it lasts this
time. That is the story. Go play nicely with your
sisters now."

"But they won't play nicely. They keep tiring
me out doing the thing you told me not to."

"How did you even learn to do such a thing

in the first place?" the other mommy asked.

"A shining person with a golden staff showed me how. She also said that the gods move in mysterious and not terribly efficient ways."

"This could be the beginning of philosophy," said the first mommy.

"You might call it that," said the other.

EXEUNT OMNES
by
Roger Zelazny

Houselights low. The Reapers & Nymphs danced as the bombs began to fall. Prospero faced Ferdinand.

" 'You do look, my son, in a mov'd sort, as if you were dismay'd. Be cheerful, sir, our revels now are ended. These our actors, as I foretold you, were all spirits, and are melted into air, into thin air . . .' "

He gestured simply. The Reapers & Nymphs vanished, to a strange, hollow and confused noise.

" '. . . And, like the baseless fabric of this vision, the cloud-capp'd towers, the gorgeous palaces, the solemn temples,' " he continued, " 'the great globe itself, yea, all which it inherit, shall dissolve and, like this insubstantial pageant faded, leave not a rack behind . . .' "

The audience vanished. The stage vanished. The theatre vanished. The city about them faded, with a strange, hollow and confused noise. The great globe itself became transparent beneath their feet. All of the actors vanished, save for the spirits of Ariel, Caliban and Prospero.

"Uh, Prossy . . ." said Ariel.

" 'We are such stuff as dreams are made on —' "

"Prospero!" bellowed Caliban.

" ' . . . And our little life is rounded with a sleep.' "

Caliban tackled him. Ariel seized him by the sleeve.

"You're doing it again, boss!"

" 'Sir, I am vexed —' "

"Stop it! The melt is on! You undid the wrong spell!"

" 'Bear with my weakness — my old brain is troubled . . .' "

Caliban sat on him. Ariel waved his slight fingers before his eyes. They drifted now in a vast and star-filled void. The nearest sizable body was the moon. Satellites — communication, astronomical, weather and spy — fled in all directions.

"Come around, damn it!" Ariel snapped. "We're all that's left again!"

" 'Be not disturbed with my infirmity . . .' "

"It's no use," growled Caliban. "He's gone off the deep end this time. What say we give up and fade away?"

"No!" Ariel cried. "I was just beginning to enjoy it.

"We are disturbed by your infirmity, Prossy! Cut the Stanislavsky bit and put things back together!"

" 'If you be pleas'd, retire into my cell and there repose . . .' "

"He's coming to the end of his lines," said Ariel. "We'll get him then."

" 'A turn or two I'll walk, to still my beating mind.' "

"Where you going to walk, boss?" Caliban asked. "You took it all away."

"Eh? What's that?"

"You did it again. It's a terrific scene that way, but it tends to be kind of final."

"Oh dear! And things are pretty far along, too."

"The farthest, I'd say, to date. What do you do for an encore?"

"Where's my Book?"

Caliban flipped his flipper.

"It went, too."

Prospero massaged his eyeballs.

"Then I'll have to work from memory. Bear with me. Where was it?"

"A desert isle."

"Yes."

He gestured magnificently and the faint outlines of palm trees appeared nearby. A slight salt scent came to them, along with the distant sounds of surf. The outlines grew more substantial and a shining sand was spread beneath their feet. There came the cry of a gull. The stars faded, the sky grew blue and clouds drifted across it.

"That's better."

"But — This is a *real* desert isle!"

"Don't argue with him. You know how he gets."

"Now, where were we?"

"The entertainment, sir."

"Ah, yes. Come to my cave. Ferdinand and Miranda will be waiting."

He led them along the shore and up to a rocky place. They entered a great grotto where a large playing area was illuminated by torchlight. Prospero nodded to Ferdinand and Miranda and gestured toward the stage.

"Boss, something's wrong."

"No tongue! all eyes! Be silent!"

Ariel lost his power of speech for the moment and regarded the scene which appeared before him.

The great globe of the Earth, sundappled, cloudstreaked, green, gray and blue, turned slowly above the playing area. Tiny sparks, missiles streaked above it, vanishing to be replaced by minute puffs of smoke over the major cities of North America, Europe and Asia. The globe rushed toward them then, one puff growing larger than the others, replacing all else. Up through dust, fire and smoke the vision swam, of a city twisted, melted, charred, its people dead, dying, fleeing.

"Boss! This is the wrong bit!" Caliban cried.

"My God!" said Ferdinand.

" 'You do look, my son, in a mov'd sort, as if you were dismay'd,' " Prospero stated.

"Here we go again," said Ariel, as the world rotated and entire land masses began to burn.

" '. . . the gorgeous palaces, the solemn temples, the great globe itself . . .' "

More missiles crisscrossed frantically as the icecaps melted and the oceans began to seethe.

" '. . . shall dissolve . . .' "

Large portions of the land were now inundated by the boiling seas.

" '. . . leave not a rack behind . . .' "

"We're still substantial," Ariel gasped.

"But it's going," Caliban observed.

The globe grew less tangible, the fires faded,

the water lost its colors. The entire prospect paled and dwindled.

" '. . . is rounded with a sleep.' " Prospero yawned.

. . . Was gone.

"Boss! What happened to —"

"Sh!" Ariel cautioned. "Don't stir him up. — Prossy, where's the theatre?"

" '. . . to still my beating mind.' "

" 'We wish your peace,' " Ferdinand and Miranda said in unison as they exited.

"Where are we, sir?"

"Why, you told me 'twas a desert isle."

"And such it is."

"Then what else would you? Find us food and drink. The other's but a dream."

"But, sir! Your Book —"

"Book me no books! I'd eat and sleep, I'd let these lovers woo, then off to Naples. All magics I eschew!"

Caliban and Ariel retreated.

"We'd best his will observe and then away."

"Aye, sprite. Methinks the living lies this way."

[*Exeunt omnes.*]

SUNGRAB
by
William F. Nolan

Sherlock Holmes was spitting up.

"Gaaa, gaa," he said, eyes rolling in his leonine skull.

"What's wrong with him now?" I asked Watson.

"A temporary regression to infancy," said the soft-voiced doctor, carefully wiping a bubble of saliva from the great detective's chin.

I scowled, kicking open a flowcab for the office bottle. "How can he regress to what he never *was*?"

"Holmes is equipped with programmed tapes extending back to a womb state. His powers of deductive reasoning must embrace the full spectrum of life." Watson stroked his pale mustache. "I, too, retain memories of a childhood I never actually experienced."

"I think Albin is overdoing things with you robos," I said, pouring myself a solid shot from the bottle.

"You are paying for the services of a master detective," Watson said, whacking Holmes sharply on the right side of the head. "Advanced robotic design is therefore essential."

Holmes blinked rapidly. A thin smile replaced the look of infant blankness. "Ah, my dear Watson," he said, drawing a heavy black pistol from the folds of his Inverness cape and pointing the gun at me. "It seems we have finally bagged our game! The infamous Moriarty is ours!"

I scowled at Watson. "He's still wacko. Tell him who I am before he fires that bloody antique!"

The good doctor leaned close to Holmes. "This is Samuel Space. He is a private investigator, and we are in his office on Mars. He has rented us to work with him."

"Yeah," I nodded. "Fifty solarcreds a day, and look what I get!"

"Stand aside, Watson!" ordered Holmes, keeping the pistol aimed at my chest. "This arch-fiend is a master of disguise, and has cleverly chosen to portray a cheap, shabbily-clad private operative of limited intelligence and inferior vocabulary in order to mask his true identity!"

"Shabbily clad!" I snapped. "I bought this zip-suit two weeks ago on Mercury — and the shirt's a pop-cuff self-wash from Allnew York." To Watson: "Better crack him again."

The mustached doctor palm-whacked Holmes once more, this time on the *left* side of his head.

Holmes gulped, slipping the gun back into his cape. He replaced it with a curving deep-bowled antique pipe, into which he tamped a rare blend of mutated Turko-Greek Earthtobacco. He puffed, expelling a cloud of aromatic intensity, regarding me with languid eyes. "I have analysed the fragment of crushed leaf-mold from the riding boot of Lady Wheatshire, and you will be pleased to know, Mr. Space, that I have *solved* the Case of the Missing Claw."

"Hey, wait a sec!" I started to protest, but Holmes silenced me with an upraised hand.

"The jeweled bird we *assumed* was in the hands of Lord Willard Wheatshire was, in actuality, never in his possession during his tenure at Suffox Hall. In a shameless yet clever act of duplicity, perpetrated by Lady Wheatshire *prior* to the time of their arrival in Suffox, a fake bird, with the *left* claw removed, was substituted — while the *genuine* Egyptian Eagle, with the worthless *right* claw missing, was passed to the blind hunchbacked gardener called Fedor, who was, of course, none other than the dastardly Mayfair pederast known as the Earl of Clax."

"Look, I —" But my words were ignored as Holmes' voice rose in triumph: "Ergo — Clax had the Claw — the *left* claw containing, within its taloned grip, the Blood Pearl of the Bonfidinis which was . . ." and he dramatically spaced his words, "never — actually — missing — at — all!"

"Brilliant!" breathed Watson, his mustache trembling. He clapped Holmes on the shoulder. "Absolutely brilliant, old fellow!"

"Except it's the wrong case," I said. "I rented you two wackos to help me solve the Saturn Time-Machine Swindle, remember?"

Watson shrugged, looking at me with sheepish, haggard eyes.

I put the office bottle away. "C'mon," I said,

grabbing my classic hat. "I'm takin' you two tin bozos back to Hu Albin's Amazing Automated Crime Clinic and get a refund."

Which is what I did. The next thing I did was vidphone my client on Saturn and admit I couldn't crack the time-machine caper.

You can't win 'em all.

Maybe I'd better tell you a little about myself. I'm an Earth op, working Big Red. I've kicked around the System from Pluto to the Moons of Mercury, but now my base is the big red one, Mars, right here in Bubble City. My office in the Boor Building is a little worn at the edges; it wouldn't cop any design awards. Neither would the cheap fleahut I rent on Redsand Avenue, but it's all I can afford on the limited solarbread I earn. I'm a barely-surviving member of a vanishing breed — what you might call the last of the private eyes. It's a bum's game. Even in its heyday this racket never paid much, but my great-grampa was a private Earthdick back in Old Los Angeles in the 20th Century so I guess it runs in the blood.

But let's get back to the case at hand . . .

Here I am, half-swacked on Moonjuice, leaving the Happy Hours Alcoholic Emporium after that vidcall to my erstwhile client.

I didn't want to go home because home was a cramped lifeunit full of Martian sandflies and broken dreams — if you'll pardon a poetic reference to personal despair. My last pairmate had walked on me three Marsmonths ago, claiming that our relationship lacked sexual intensity. She was right. I'd used up most of my sexual intensity on a Venusian triplehead during a multi-operational star-dodge tax fraud assignment on Ganymede.

So my unit was empty now — just me and the sandflies — which explains why I was in no big rush to get back there on this particular evening.

I needed a prime brainblast — a full sensory vacation from the lousy detective biz — so I found the nearest Mindmaze, zipped myself into a Tripchair, snapped on the lobe pads, and blasted.

I was deeped, clam-happy, really into it, when an abrupt powerbreak made me surface.

I blinked up at a tall, cat-eyed Earthgirl in a tiger-striped wig. She was poured into a tri-glo slimsuit and knee-high lifeleather bootkins. An absolute knockout.

"I'm sorry I broke your contact," she said, facing my chair, looking very determined, "but I knew you wouldn't be back in your office before morning and I had to see you now."

"You could have let me finish my blast," I said, popping my pads and leaving the Tripchair.

"This matter is quite urgent, Mr. Space."

"You know me, but I don't know you."

"Amanda Nightbird," she said. "I shake with the Saints."

"Right," I said. "I've seen you on the vids. How'd you get my name?"

"You were recommended by a friend as a reliable private hop," she said.

"Private op," I corrected. "Short for individual operative."

"The term is not familiar," she told me.

"That's because there aren't many of us around anymore."

"Anyhow," she said with impatience, "I know what you do and I want you to do it."

"Do what, Miss Nightbird?"

"Protect. You do protect people, don't you? . . . I mean, isn't that part of what you do as a . . . private whatever?"

"Sure," I nodded. "Protection's in my line. Two hundred solarcreds a day, plus expenses. Now, just who do I protect?"

"Me," said the girl with a shake of her tiger hair.

"And when do I begin?"

"Now," she said, nodding toward the exit. "There's something outside, waiting to kill me!"

She was accurate; it wasn't "someone" — it was "something." A nine-foot multi-armed spider assassin from the Rings of Orion. I was ready for him when he dropped from the roof onto the person he thought was Amanda Nightbird.

He got a royal shock: I was wearing Amanda's tiger-striped wig, knee-high lifeleather bootkins and tri-glo slimsuit. Amanda remained inside the building in her skimpies.

I'm trained in seventeen forms of solar combat, so when this spider guy landed on my lower back (planning to sink his poison fangs in my neck — or, to be precise, into Amanda's neck) I dipped into a lateral reverse Mercurian half-twist and sent him flying. Before he could regain balance I delivered a neatly-executed double heel snap to his upper mandibles. Hissing, he lunged at me again — but by this time I had my .38 nitrocharge fingergrip Colt-Wesson out and working for me. I re-distributed his atoms, blasting him into a multitude of hairy black pieces. (Universal law: nothing ever dies in the cosmos.)

Then I went back inside and asked Amanda Nightbird why a spider assassin from Orion was trying to kill her.

She wore glitternip on her breasts, and looked so great in her skimpies, with her perfect skin shining in the semi-gloom, that I found it difficult to concentrate on her reply — but it had to do with a risk-debt she's refused to pay after losing to a rigged Gravgame at Honest Al's Pleasure Palace.

"I know Al," I told her, squeezing her right breast. "I can square it for you."

"He's a crook!" she said with heat. "I wish you wouldn't."

"Square it?"

"No, squeeze my breast. I don't like them pinched or squeezed. My first bedmate did that and it absolutely ruined our pairup. I like them flat-palmed or caressed lightly around the inner aureole."

"Oke," I said, handing over her tiger-striped wig. "But you do want me to fix things with Al?"

"Oh, yes, I do," she said as I passed her clothes back to her. "But I refuse to pay him a thousand creds when I know he manipulated the gravity field on that spinwheel."

"Gotcha," I agreed, watching her slide into her slimsuit.

"There's something else," she said, looking up at me with deep-lashed eyes. "What do you know about the meaning of dreams?"

"I'm an op not a headpsyc," I said. "What kind of dreams?"

"Nightmares. I keep dreaming that frost is everywhere, freezing all life. Over and over lately . . . the same dream. What do you make of it?"

I was watching her tab her bootkins when I realized we were cosmically destined to pairmate.

"I'll have to pass on the meaning of your dreams," I told her. "But I'm convinced we're prime pairmate material. What say?"

Her eyes cat-flashed. "You *are* attractive," she agreed. "But our body-jag will have to wait. I'm due with the Saints — for a shake sesh on the Marble, and you have to square me with Honest Al."

"Ummmmm," I said.

"How much is all this going to cost me?"

"No way to tell," I said. "Depends on what I can do with Al."

"I trust you, Sam." Her voice was a purr as I flat-palmed her right breast. "My future rests with you."

I knew that cosmic destiny could be depended upon. Somewhere in the multi-layered swiss cheese of the universe, in a counter-dimensional reality, we were already body-jagging like crazy.

I looked forward to it.

Honest Al's was located just beyond Mars, on a runt-sized private asteroid called Burton's Rock, which was a quick hop from Bubble City. The Rock got a lot of local action since Gambledens were illegal in B City. I'd been there often enough to know my way around, and I was never dumb enough to buck a spinwheel. I stuck to mag craps. At least you can't rig a set of magnetic dice, so all you had to beat were house odds. Sometimes I got lucky . . .

You couldn't miss Al's joint; it was set smack into the fat lip of a big radioactive crater. You could see the glow for miles coming in from the dark side of Mars.

Inside, Al's Pleasure Palace was no palace. Al kept the upkeep down and play-profits up; he didn't need high gloss to attract the suckers. I spotted him at a corner drinktable with two fleekers from the Capella System. Al was buttering them up for a big spend. Fleeks have a natural urge for high-stakes action, which Al happily encouraged.

I walked over to his table.

"Samuel!" he beamed. "How jolly to see you again!"

"We need to talk," I said, tight-voiced. "*Alone*."

The two fleeks looked up at me with lidless orbs.

"Later, Samuel. I'm with friends."

Al was big, maybe three hundred Earthpounds, and his tri-color changesuit didn't flatter his bulk. I put my left thumb against the upper ridge of his bloated neck, applied pressure. He grunted in sudden pain.

"We talk *now*," I said. "You two . . . Up!"

The fleeks wavered to their feet; a fleek panics easy. They don't like violence in any form.

"Frap off!" I told them. And they waddled away, their stalk eyes bugged in fear.

I took my thumb out of Al's neck and sat down.

"What'll you have?" asked the drinktable. I

ordered a double Irish, no cubes. Al was glaring at me, his wide face flushed and beaded with sweat bubbles.

"I could have you iced for this," he said tightly. His eyes were smoked steel with heat in the center. I grinned at him.

"You're real good at having people iced," I said. "That's why I'm here."

"Huh?" He blinked at me.

"You put out the killword on a Saint, and she came to me. I told her I'd have it canceled."

"You told her wrong, peeper," said Al. "She owes. She won't pay. She dies. One-two-three."

I shook my head slowly. "She was stiffed on a rigged spin, and you know it," I said. "Either you call off the hounds or I bring this seedy joint down around your fat pink ears!"

I sipped my Irish as Al thought that one over.

"You're running a bluff, Sam," he said, but his voice lacked conviction.

I gestured toward a vidphone near the bar. "Try me. One call to my ole buddy, Solarpolice Captain Shaun O'Malloy telling him what I know about your sleazy operation and you're out of biz." I leaned close to Al's sweating face. "Cancel the word on my client, or I cancel your whole operation."

Then I sat back and lit a cigar. Al let out a long sigh, raised a fat hand. One of his boys glided to the table, giving me a hard lookover. Al snapped out two words: "Nightbird lives."

The goon nodded and slid back into the crowd.

"Thanks," I said to Al. "That was a real sweet thing to do."

But Al was still sweating; I wondered why.

"Look, Sam . . ." His voice was soft. "There's more to this than wheelmoney. I was under orders. The debt was just a cover. Take my word and stay clear of her. She's going down, Sam. One way or another."

I'd never seen Al like this. He was gut-scared.

"Tell me about it," I said. "*All* of it. Who hired you to kill the girl? And why?"

He looked up at me with agonized eyes. His jowls were quivering. "I tell you — and I'm dead, Sam. Just like her."

"Nobody has to know you told me anything."

"It's too dangerous. I only said what I did to keep you out of it."

"No good, Al. I'm *in* it. Now *spill!*"

His voice went all whispery; I could barely make out the words: "Amanda knows something she shouldn't . . . about the Big Lizard."

"Stanton P. Henshaw, the onion magnate?"

Al nodded. "She was hired for one of his bash-parties on Pluto — with the Saints. They were doing a shake up there that night and between sessions Amanda wandered into the gardens next to the main poolhouse. She overheard Henshaw. He was with some galactic highwigs. She heard them talking."

"About what?"

"Dunno, but something big," Al whispered. "Big enough for Henshaw to hire me to get a job done on Amanda Nightbird. I rigged the grav-game, and after she lost at the wheel I *let* her find out about the rig. I knew she'd refuse to pay — which gave me the excuse I needed to put out the killword. She doesn't know the *real* reason."

"But if she heard something important enough to scare the Big Lizard wouldn't she have *told* someone?"

Al's voice became even more intense: "That's just it, Sam . . . she doesn't *know* she knows what she knows!"

"Run that by me again."

"What she actually overheard has been erased from her conscious mind. Henshaw deeped her before she left Pluto — so the words now exist *only* in her subconscious. But a police data-scan could reveal those words, and the Lizard wants her dead."

"Then why didn't he kill her himself?"

Al shook his fleshy head. "Couldn't afford the risk. Everyone knew she was shaking at his place that night. He had to make sure her death wouldn't tie in to him — and that's why he contacted *me* for the ice job."

I leaned back, twisting my classic hat in my hands. "The question is — just *what* did she overhear?"

"I swear you don't want to know," Al said. "Just like *I* don't want to know. Sure, I'll call off the kill, but it won't save her. When she walked into that garden she bought herself a ticket to the boneyard, and you can't save her. Stay out of it, Sam. Nobody fraps around with the Big Lizard."

"Just let me worry about that slimy green bastard!"

"But when he finds out I've called in the word . . . he'll . . ."

"He won't do anything. We'll nail him first."

Al's thick eyebrows raised. "We?"

"Me and Shaun O'Malloy. The Captain's had a long line out on Henshaw's scaly hide. My guess is that whatever's inside Amanda's head will provide the hook he needs to pull in the Lizard!"

After leaving Al's I booked an express-warper for Jupiter. I had to locate Amanda fast and get her to O'Malloy at Solar HQ in Allnew York. I'd have him run a brainscan to uncover what she knew.

The police in ten Systems had been after Stanton Henshaw, but — until now — the Big Lizard had been arrest-proof. Sure, every gumshoe in the galaxy knew how crooked he was, knew that his onion empire was just a legit cover for his monumentally corrupt activities, but without hard evidence he was beyond the law's reach. Now, thanks to private operative Samuel T. Space, the Big Boy was about to be netted.

It was a real sweet setup, and I was making it all happen.

When we touched down on the Marble I hailed an airkab for Juketown. I knew she was shaking with the Saints at the Bent Tentacle, an upperclass drinkdive in the heart of town. Most of the hot off-planet acts played there — and the Saints were steaming. Their tri-disc of "Ionized Particle Blues" was numero uno on the starcharts.

At the club they told me she was doing a celeb vidstint as a guest panelist at KRAB, the local Tri-Vid Station. Her appearance was slated as prime PR for the Saints, and the manager of the club was happy to provide me with a free ticket. When I got there the show was already in full gear. The panelists were heavily into a discussion of cosmic sexual customs. A purple twinhead from Antar, with mottled chestfarbs, was yelling stridently at a tri-tongued toadwoman from Capella.

Amanda was at the far right, looking terrific in thighslash trimtops; she was the only Earthfem on the panel.

"Are you trying to tell me, Miss Penzler, that satisfactory intercourse is possible with a single penis?" the twinhead bellowed.

"Absolutely!" the toadwoman yelled back. "Just because the males on your planet have two heads and three pricks you assume an offensive air of sexual superiority!"

"Talk about offensive!" countered the twinhead. "At least I don't publicly refer to a male's sex organ as a 'prick' . . ."

"Ladies, ladies — let's have order!" shouted the moderator, a reedskin from the Dogstar System. His snaky tail bristled with dignity.

A testy silence settled over the panelists.

"I think we should let Miss Amanda Nightbird, our panelist from Earth, respond to Miss Grinstead's question," said the moderator, nodding toward Amanda.

"Well, I really don't have a great deal of multipenis experience," she admitted. "But, to quote the ancient saying: 'It ain't no matter who owns the store, it's how you use the merchandise.' At least I —"

"No, no, that's not how it goes," cut in a fourth panel member, a feathered tri-sexual from Titan. "It's 'Never mind the mishkas, just deliver the mulligan!' That's how it goes!"

This touched off a bitter shouting match between the three off-Earth panelists, which was finally terminated by the agitated moderator, who declared the discussion at an end.

The Tri-Vid cameras were still on Amanda as she left the station, so I had to wait until she reached the liftlot outside KRAB before approaching her.

She was startled to see me.

"Sam! What are you doing here? I thought you were squaring me with Honest Al."

"That's done — but it isn't over."

"I don't understand."

An airkab touched down next to us, and I pushed her inside.

"Launchport," I told the kab.

"But I'm due back at the club!"

"Nix on that. We've got to see O'Malloy in Allnew York."

"The solar cop?"

"Yep. He doesn't like private ops, but when I bring you in he's gonna love me!"

Her eyes flashed anger. "I have no intention of going to Allnew York with you. I shake tonight at the Tentacle."

"I didn't figure you'd want to go, and I haven't got time to argue, so . . ." I pressed a spot just at the base of Amanda's skull. Her eyes saucered, she let out a small sigh — and slumped loosely against my shoulder.

So far, so good.

When we reached Earth Amanda was totally zonked: I'd slipped her some L-17 on the flight, and I had to carry her into Solar HQ. When I

located O'Malloy I told him to break out the
brain-scan equipment, that we had a prime can-
didate for a Reading.

He didn't see it that way.

"Space, you're under arrest," he told me, spitting out the words around a cigar the size of a
NewTexas fencepost. He was tall and wide and
tough — and he seemed to enjoy glaring at people.

I glared back, into his steamed Irish face: "On
what charge?"

"Kidnapping," snapped O'Malloy. "You admit
you took Miss Nightbird off Jupiter in a disabled
condition without her free consent?"

"Sure I admit it, but I brought her directly to
you, didn't I?"

"It's not *where* you brought her, it's *how* you
brought her! She's still zonked. We can't get a
word out of her."

Several other solarcops, equally tough, lounged
around the captain's office, giving me the sour
eye. The place smelled of stale sweat and cigar
smoke. The coolvents were jammed, and the
room was windowless.

"The words you want are all locked in her subconscious," I told O'Malloy. "Just do what I *said*,
run a mind-scan on her."

"I don't take orders from sleazy, lowlife private
snoops," growled the tall Irishman. "I'll decide
on a scan — depending on what Miss Nightbird
has to say when she norms out."

"I gave her L-17. That's strong stuff. If you wait
till she's back to normal we might lose the Big
Lizard."

"We?" O'Malloy stumped out his massive

weed against the side of his nearwood desk and ambled over to me. I was in a holdchair, facing the desk, and he leaned down to cup my chin in a beefy paw. "There's no 'we' in this case, there's only *me!* If the Lizard gets nailed, I nail him."

He uncupped my chin, walked back to his desk and slid into his nearleather swivchair. "Okay, Sammy," he said, "I'll take a chance and play it your way." O'Malloy leaned forward, eyes hard and glittering. "But it better pay off . . . It just *better!*"

I'd never witnessed a scan, so it was all new to me.

The Reading Room was small and white and sterile. Two robos moved inside as we watched the action through a transview-wall. Amanda, still out of it, was webbed into the Bodytable and a faceless robo was attaching brainpads to her skull. A second faceless robo handled the Scanner — a large, floor-to-ceiling console filling one side of the chamber.

"How come we're not allowed inside?" I asked O'Malloy.

"A scan requires isolation," he said. "The isometric electrovibrations would be affected if any other brains were in the room." O'Malloy thumbed a speakswitch. "You can begin."

The lights inside dimmed to black as Amanda's skull began to glow; I could see her brain inside, like Jello in a bowl, pulsing with light.

"Sub-con level achieved," reported the console robo.

"Scan," ordered O'Malloy.

Words flashed in erratic patterns across the

console's scan-screen, words deep-buried in Amanda Nightbird's subconscious:

... CAN DO IT? ... YES ... HAVE THE POWER ... TOW INTO NEW ORBIT ... WITHOUT SUN ... SYSTEM DIES ...

The words went on, revealing Stanton P. Henshaw's plan as totally monstrous: using a newly-developed Moon Machine, the Big Lizard intended to steal our Sun, tow it into a new orbit outside the System, and put its vast solar energy to his own infernal purpose, as fuel for a destructive Device so powerful that Sol itself was needed to power it! With this Device he could control most of the Milky Way!

The words spilled out of Amanda's mind onto the screen as she lay, serene of feature, eyes closed, totally unaware of the incredible data she was giving us.

No wonder Stanton P. Henshaw wanted her dead!

"Now I know what her dreams really meant," I told O'Malloy.

"Dreams?"

"Nightmares about frost being everywhere, freezing all life ... With ole Sol towed away things would get damned chilly!"

O'Malloy stared at me, shaken. "Can he *do* it, Sam? ... Can he grab our Sun?"

I nodded. "Sure. Unless he's stopped."

"But how?" O'Malloy slammed a beefy fist against the wall. "If I nab him his lawboys will have him sprung before I can spit! We need to have proof! We need to find out where that Moon Machine of his is stashed!"

"Obviously on a Moon outside our System," I said. "But which?"

"Yeah . . . *which?*" He scowled. "We need more than some words inside a dame's head to shut down the Lizard!"

"Then I'll get what you need," I promised O'Malloy. "We know the Lizard has an Onion Palace near Alpha Centauri. I can infiltrate the Palace and get our proof. A plan like this is bound to be fully documented. I'll bring back what you need to nail him."

"Just remember one thing," said the big Irishman. "If you die, the System dies with you."

A commercial starliner got me into the Alpha Centauri System, but I wasn't riding as a paid passenger. I arrived at Henshaw's in a *box* — as one of a houseserve squad of work robos, part of an exchange shipment. His old work robos were to be picked up for restoration, replaced by these new models.

I knew that my robo disguise was flawless, but I was a bit apprehensive as the Froggie Housemom released me from my insulated Pac-crate.

"Name, origin and work specialty," snapped the tall froggie. She was soot-green and stalk-eyed, like all froggies, with the usual spotted stomach and big flat wet eyes. I never liked froggies. They're naturally vicious and anti-social, which is one of the reasons the Big Lizard employed them.

"Speak up!" she demanded.

My bulbeyes blinked at her; a metalspeak altered my voice tone: "Name: Ernesto. Origin: the Earthcoast of Sicily."

"Specialty?"

"I am a faxcab refurbisher," I told her.

She jabbed that info into her punchsheet, nodding her spadeshaped green head.

I was being very clever, since I knew that Henshaw never took the risk of sending his faxfile cabinets out for refurbishing. It was an in-Palace project. The robo I'd replaced in the shipment had been programmed to handle this job — which gave me easy entry to the Lizard's personal files.

And I was fully prepared: my left eye housed a minicam, operated by blinking the bulb on my right eye. I could shoot faxphotos as fast as I could blink.

I was grinning behind my faceplate as I walked into Henshaw's Palace. It took genius to pull off a caper like this.

My kind of genius.

By the end of the first workperiod I'd cased the whole setup: the faxfiles, method of data-storage, location of primary info. I waited until the work shutdown, when all the robos were de-activated, before making my move. The Housemom was off-duty, and it was a cinch to slip past the corridor guard.

Inside the faxroom, I did a quick computo-check on primary data and — presto! Jackpot! There it was: Henshaw's full Sungrab plan. I got it all, minicam whirring, and was slotting it back into the proper cab when I heard a slithering sound directly behind me. I spun around, going for the .38 under my chestplate, but I wasn't fast enough. The gun was tongue-snapped from my hand before I could squeeze the trigger. A froggie nightguard faced me, snapping a set of nippers over my wrists.

"Let me go and you're a rich reptile," I told him. "You can retire from this racket."

He watched me with yellow eyes, his tongue flicking against his thin lips. Froggies are incredibly fast with those long sharp tongues of theirs, and I didn't need another demonstration. He wasn't buying the bribe.

"Mom wants to see you," he hissed.

The Housemom's room was as green as she was — a color I never much cared for. U.S. Earthmoney used to be green, back in the Twentieth Century, until the first woman president took office in 1999. She got the Pink Act through Congress and after that money was a lot prettier. Funny, the thoughts that jump through your mind in a state of crisis . . .

"Did you really think I'd be fooled by your clumsy disguise?" the Housemom asked.

"I — don't know what you mean," I said. "It is obvious that I am a sturdisteel J-4 work robo manufactured for commercial cleanup within the System. My work number is 555563249." I dropped my pants — showing her the number which was stamped into my left buttplate.

She circled me. "And what kind of work robo packs a .38?"

I sighed, having no answer for that one.

In one swift, clawing motion she ripped loose my fake chestplate, revealing pale Earthskin. "Ugh!" she grunted. "How *revolting!*"

"Yeah — well, green scales don't do anything for me, sister!"

And, with that, I reached between my teeth,

plucked out the tooth-laser I'd taped to the roof
of my mouth, and shot her head off.

She made an ugly green puddle at my feet.

I'd learned something in the faxroom. I'd
learned that the Moon Machine wasn't on any
moon. Moon stood for Multi Operational Orbit
Neutralizer — and the Machine was right smack
dab under my nose, in the sub-basement of Henshaw's Palace.

I took a dropchute down there.

Things were getting a bit tight, since the Lizard's plan indicated that he was set to begin his
solar tow job any minute now. No time to get
back to O'Malloy. I couldn't depend on the cops
to stop Stanton P. Henshaw; I'd have to stop him
personally.

He was just where I thought he'd be — inside
the Machine, at the controls, preparing to launch
Operation Sungrab.

Getting in there wasn't easy: I had to gun down
three froggies to clear the Machine, then set my
.38 at full thrust to cut my way inside. The mi-
croblast ripped a hole in the wall of the Machine
large enough for me to jump through.

I jumped — taking the onion magnate by surprise. He lunged at me from the control board,
an electro-kickstick in his webbed paw. I jerked
sideways, but the stick caught me on the upper
right shoulder and my arm exploded into pain.
The .38 dropped from my numbed fingers as we
circled each other.

On the viewscreen I caught a quick glimpse of
our Sun, slowly being sucked into space. It was
too late: he was killing the System!

"I am a private operative representing the solar

police," I warned Henshaw. "Surrender now, and you won't be hurt."

Henshaw let out a short, barking lizard's laugh. "Your solar system will soon be nothing but so many balls of ice." He kept circling me. "You were exceedingly stupid to come here alone. Did you *really* except to take me back to Earth?"

"I'll take you back," I promised, and with a brilliantly timed Venusian twist-kick I sent the electrostick spinning from his claw.

They didn't call him the Big Lizard for laughs; he *was* big, over eight feet from the top of his leathery head to the tip of his scaly tail. His daggered teeth, flat-black lizard eyes and hairy green ears were anything but attractive. He wore a tucked-velvet tuxedo, topped by a handsome neckscarf of cross-woven silk which failed to offset his basic grossness. Ugly is ugly — and Stanton P. Henshaw was one ugly lizard.

Henshaw didn't say anything more; his flat eyes glistened with fury as he came at me, claws extended. I dropped to one knee and used the tried-and-true Mercurian headbutt — which sent the big guy reeling back, off-balance and vulnerable to a Saturnian wrist-lock. His eyes bulged as I applied pressure.

"Gotcha!" I said.

I was wrong. A giant onion swung from his neck on a looped chain, and using a free claw he pushed the onion into my face.

I did the natural thing: I burst into tears.

Sobbing, I found myself slammed to the closemarble floor, a wide green lizard's foot on my neck.

"You see," he hissed. "I don't need the help of my froggies in attending to you. In another micromoment your neck will snap like a Plutonian breadstick under my foot!"

And it would have — except for the fact that I was able to grab Henshaw's hanging appendage. I jerked downward with full strength and the Big Lizard let out a howl and staggered back, tail lashing in agony. No reptile I know of, on any planet, likes to have his appendage jerked.

While he howled and hopped I scooped up my .38 and laid the barrel across his skull. Which put him to sleep.

A quick glance at the screen told me ole Sol was being sucked deeper into space — and I had to stop it, fast.

The controls weren't all that tough to figure out, and I was able to reverse the Sun's direction, slowly guiding it back into its proper solar orbit . . .

Then I locked down the shutoffs and set the Machine at Self-Destruct.

Before it blew Henshaw's Palace into ten billion atomized fragments I was heading back to Allnew York in the onion magnate's personal starhopper.

And strapped into the flyseat next to me, still sleeping like a babe, was the big boy himself.

Sam, I told myself, you're a bloody marvel!

O'Malloy looked terrible when I walked into his office with the Lizard in tow.

The captain was blue; his teeth were chattering and the hairs inside his nose were frozen. A thin film of white frost covered the walls, floor and the top of O'Malloy's desk — and all of the solar dicks in the room looked as bad as he did.

"S – S – S – Sam," he chattered. "G – G – G – Great work!"

"Thanks," I grinned. "I took minicam shots of everything you need to put the Lizard on ice." Then I realized that the term was inappropriate in these circumstances. "Uh . . . look, you'll heat up soon, Cap. I got the Sun back into orbit before I left. Just take a while to thaw things out."

"That's f – f – f – fine," said O'Malloy.

When it was over, with the Lizard locked up and the Sun warm in the sky, I took Amanda back to my lifeunit in Bubble City for our body-jag.

We were jagging like crazy when Sherlock Holmes walked in. "How careless of you, my dear Moriarty, leaving your door unlocked. It will doubtless be your last mistake!" He had his pistol out, pointed at me. "Please stand clear of the young woman," he ordered. "And place your hands atop your head."

I hopped from the jumpbed, starkers, hands on head. When a wacky robo with an antique pistol gives me an order I obey it.

"Who is this maniac?" Amanda demanded to know.

"He's from the Hu Albin Amazing Automated Crime Clinic," I told her. "And he thinks I'm a master criminal."

"This is ridiculous," she snorted.

"I've tracked this fiend halfway round the world," Holmes said to Amanda. "Now, at last, he's in my hands!"

"Not quite, old fellow," said a voice behind Holmes. It was Hu Albin, and he was pointing a laser cannon at the great detective. "Now, give me that pistol!"

Holmes turned slowly, let out a long sigh, and handed over the gun. Hu Albin then pressed a button in the robo's neck, and Holmes became motionless.

"Sorry about this, Mr. Space," said Hu Albin. "He's on the fritz again. I'm having him completely rewired."

Amanda and I were standing there, both starkers, staring at Albin. "Get out," I said in a hard tone. "And take that wacked-out tinman with you."

"Of course," nodded Albin, flushing. He pressed another button on the robot, and Holmes meekly padded out, followed by Albin.

I turned to Amanda, but she was dressing. "Hey," I said. "What goes?"

"*I* go!" she snapped. "The jag's over, Sam. Enough is enough. My nerves can't take any more. Your lifestyle is just too erratic."

And she left me. Just like that.

I was alone. Ole Sam, last of the private eyes. Alone again. Well, not quite.

I still had the Martian sandflies.

And a lot of broken dreams.

WHERE ARE YOU NOW, ERIK SCORBIC?

by
K. Copeland Shea

The last man born on Earth was a half-wit; the other half — that part of his mind which was not of this world — was often away, somewhere else. Exactly where, nobody knew, for when he was there the rest of him seemed so serene, so beatific, that no one dared to disturb him by asking, not even in whisper, "Where are you now, Erik Scorbic?" And when he came back he did not know that he'd been away, much less remember where he had gone or what he'd done there. But the reluctance with which he made his reentry into mundane reality was enough to indicate that all was not nearly as well with the world as it was with the somewhere else.

Dr. Only's diagnosis: senilism.

"What for heaven's sake is senilism?" asked the mother.

"Premature senility."

"What! At the age of two?"

It was the media that had made such a thing

of him, made a hero of him just for having been born.

By the time Erik had been three months in the womb, the first flurry of concern over the future of mankind was flying thick and fast: DOCTORS REPORT DRASTIC RISE IN SPONTANEOUS ABORTIONS. HOSPITALS CROWDED WITH D.&C. PATIENTS. W.H.O. REGISTERS CONSTERNATION. Then, the storm of speculation: VIRUS? FLUORIDE? RADIATION? GERM WARFARE? PSYCHIC EPIDEMIC? MASS HYPNOSIS? ACT OF GOD?

On Dec. 2, 1991, a *New York Times* report indicated that no human births had been registered anywhere in the world since March 4 of that year, when Annabelle Wong was born in Peking. Furthermore, the number of pregnancies in the first trimester was down to 64% of the statistics of the year before; the number of pregnancies in the second and third trimesters was zero. The article was headlined, IS THIS THE BEGINNING OF THE END OF THE WORLD?

It was the first time anyone had said it aloud.

The next day, Erik was born to Roger and Anna Scorbic of 27 Appletree Drive, Annapolis, Md., U.S.A. It was a complete surprise to them both. Anna, who had been barren for all of her 52 years, had assumed that the oddities which had visited her body during the last few months were due to change-of-life. The slight swelling of her already ample abdomen was assigned to an excess of pickles. And it was what she described as an acute attack of wind which blew her to the hospital and into the operating room. There, before they could open her up, Erik found his own way out — all three pounds of him. He took one look at the swollen veins of his mother's thighs and screamed in horror at the haplessness of life.

Anna was amazed to find him there; but for the umbilical cord, she would never have claimed him as her own.

Roger refused to claim him at all, "Who would believe it after all these years?" He left home on the effluvia of moral indigestion.

Anna didn't mind. She had her Erik — when he was there at all. Also plenty of publicity. And free samples of just about everything.

The first thing Erik ever said — on the occasion of his third birthday — was, "Gone are the days that were; here come the days that weren't and nevermore shall be, so!"

There were witnesses, not only the guests but at least a dozen reporters. With the knife poised above his birthday cake, Erik paused only long enough to make his pronouncement. Then he hacked the cake to bits.

If he had been any other imbecile, the world would not have listened to such fatuity. But as the probable last of humankind, he was instantaneously deified into the living oracle of the future, of what was left of the future. And, as such, his words were sacrosanct, open though they were to profane interpretation.

During the course of the next year and a half, Erik was known to utter three more phrases; otherwise, he made no sounds at all except to squeak in appreciation when his mother served him tapioca pudding, five times a day.

In March of 1995, as he spooned hot applesauce into his uncle's boot, Erik muttered, "Hot is hot and cold is not, then the twain shall be the same."

On the seventh of August of that year he said to the postman, "If you paint the sky a different color every day, after awhile it will forget that really it is only blue."

In February of 1996, the next oracle was given privately to his mother in such a confidential — almost conspiratorial — manner that she deliberated several days before handing it over to the rest of the world. In the end she allowed herself to relent to the persuasion of her own sophistry: Who am I to own an oracle all to myself? In reality she couldn't wait to hear what the neighbors would have to say.

She gave a tea party. "Guess what that naughty little boy of mine told me the other day," she said casually as she was passing the cashews. All the ladies stopped, some with sticky buns still stuck in their molars, others with mouthsful of tepid tea left unswallowed. "He told me," and here Anna paused for the most effect. "He said: 'High in the hills a mushroom mourns for the sheep in whose shit it is growing.'"

Always each new statement aroused controversy as to its meaning, and various schools of interpretation rose and fell on the sea of public favor. By July of 1996, at the time just before the fifth oracle, the many factions, cliques, and splinter groups had merged and submerged and re-emerged to merge again, finally to settle into the two major expository bodies which were to persist until the end of all time.

The followers of Sri Bundi called themselves Verities.

"I am Verity, who are you?"

"I am Verity too."

Verity Sri Bundi — a one-time London dock worker — taught that the sayings of The Veriest Erik Scorbic substantiated one of his own revelations: the souls of the dead were simply refusing to move into the bodies of unborn babies, striking *en masse* against reincarnating into a world so putrid with spiritual pollution. He augmented his argument by explaining that when the mind of The Veriest wandered it went to hobnob with the unemployed souls in the waiting room of the spheres — playing chess and snooker, philosophizing with the adolescent suicides, and occasionally even joining the pickets with a placard saying: BETTER DEAD THAN ED, JANE, JOHN, SALLY, OR EVEN ERIK SCORBIC, in red, white, and gold.

The Verities tithed their worldly goods to Nature and lived in small agricultural communities scattered like dandelion seeds all over the world, spending their time — the time not expended on keeping themselves alive — in preparing for death. When one of their members died they did not mourn, but rejoiced: "Verily, Verity, I say unto you, there are better worlds out there for you to go to than this one!"

The movement in juxtaposition to the Verities was presided over by the charismatic young American drive-in movie magnate, William Abbott Young. His adherents were known as the Willabies. To be a Willaby was to be a believer in the creed: If you can't save the human race, the least you can do is to save its idea of itself — in sealed units strategically placed around the world to be found by whatever intelligence comes along next. Willabies called themselves collectors of the past although, once an initial sketch of history was stowed safely away, the past tended to be mostly made up of their own present. To which they daily added excerpts from the organ newspaper, *The Willaby World.*

On July 9, 1996, *The Willaby World* reported that the "prognosticator" Erik Scorbic had said to an assemblage of Willabies at an A. A. meeting in Annapolis that, "Sooner or later the world will be as flat as it was before Columbus didn't fall off of it." W. A. Young, chairman of the board of trustees of the W. A. Young Foundation and spokesman for The Willabies of the World, was quoted as having warned that Scorbic's message was merely a reaffirmation of the end of mankind. The term "flat" was only a cryptic reference to the impalatability of a world without men, and was not to be confused with any impending rearrangement of the earth's surface; in other words, the Willaby Institute's topography department — in charge of the distribution of the information modules — was not to get itself into a dither.

Sri Bundi, the only Verity who was entrusted to read newspapers, interpreted the words of The Veriest as meaning that the world would never be any flatter than it ever had been, which was never, and that it would get along without men as well in the future as it had in the past — maybe even better, since now it knew that it was round.

He also declared that human disappearance from the earth would occur within less time than had been previously anticipated. After a brief phone call to Anna Scorbic he was able to estab-

lish that The Veriest had been misquoted as saying "sooner or later" when in fact what he had
said was "sooner than later." This was then read
to mean: sooner than would be expected in the
simple dwindling away of men if people continued to die off at the present rate, one by one, or
at least not in groups larger than could be contained in a jumbo jet.

And so this latest oracle was passed along from
one Verity community to the next by word of
mouth and the farther the word got from Sri
Bundi's mouth, the sooner the doom. It was a
comment on the strength of the Community at
large that not one person preempted his part in
the general fate of mankind by doing-in his own
individual destiny. However, there was a spate
of deaths from cholera along the upper Amazon
where the forecast was down to the year 2000,
only three and a half years away. And in Auck-
land the Verities took to taking snuff.

(The reason that the four year old Erik had been
at an A. A. meeting at all was that no one would
baby-sit for him, no one wanted to be alone with
the Oracle in case he should decide to speak. This
anticipatory fear was the same as that which had
driven Anna Scorbic to drink — mostly cooking
sherry out of a cheap sense of subtlety — and at
the same time it was her pride in her role as
mother-of-the-Oracle which drove her out every
Wednesday night to A. A., where she could brag
about him to her heart's content. "All things considered," she would sigh after expelling some
saga of indeterminable anxiety, "I just couldn't
help myself.")

Those who did not call themselves Verities or

count themselves among the Willabies simply kept their eyes closed and tried to go on as before. There were, however, more and more unavoidable things for them to bump into, and in time they too gave up living in the nonexistent future. The ones who did not die of it joined the Willabies in their search for the present.

Within a few years the chirrup of childish prattle had ceased altogether; instead, the cackle of childlike twaddle — the song of senility — was heard behind the silence. Evidently it had always been there, but no one had listened before. Now it was encouraged, at first to fill the unacknowledged void, then — as the average age crept up and up — in resigned recognition that there were proportionally more old people every day and, "One day there won't be anyone else so we might as well prepare the way for ourselves."

Gradually there was a marked change in the mode, the mood, of life. Affluence was everywhere. When many millions of Verities had first abandoned their lands and fortunes, other people had taken them up and used them as their own. Now rich men were dying without progeny and charity organizations distributed property and home-computer units the way they had once passed out food parcels.

There was too much. So that the initial greed, the gorging, the orgy was soon brought to a standstill in the quicksand inconvenience of the too much; there was no one to hire to take care of it, for everyone had his own. Not even wanton squandering, not within the fat satisfaction that there were more than enough cars, stereos, tinned foods, wine and spirits, medicines, fuel, paper,

clothing, soap powder, lipstick, textbooks, elastic
bands, etc., to sate everybody's appetite forever.

It had taken nearly a decade for the momentum
of mass production to slow down and stop.

Now life was tuned to the pursuits of leisure —
reading, films, travelling, games and sports, crafts
and art. But, in their spare time, many found
pleasure in a bit of work. All services were public,
manned by volunteers. Shops and restaurants
were run for the fun of it; usually there were as
many employees as customers, and even then the
customers would often insist on waiting on themselves. Dairy products, meats and fish, fresh fruits
and vegetables, and bakery goods, were the by-
products of hobbies. Entertainment was free for
the appreciation of it.

Only a tiny percentage of professional people
were still needed and many of those continued
with their needless work simply because they
couldn't break the habit; doctors worked half-
days and teachers worked one hour shifts, lawyers drew straws for the privilege of a case. However, journalists worked round the clock looking
for something to write about.

With less stress and more human interaction,
crime had abated, alcoholism and drug addiction
had all but disappeared. Mental illness was dras-
tically reduced; there was a plethora of little old
ladies only too eager to undo the mother-who-
never-loved-you. However, dysphoria was not
only epidemic but chronic. For awhile it was
known as "the fug," but eventually it was so common a condition that no one remembered not
having it and so there was no need to call it
anything at all. It was there nonetheless, the va-

guest malaise. Evidently the new individual integrity found in communal sharing and consideration of others did not quite compensate for the death of dreams.

With the loss of the future went the initiative, the will, to go on to beyond. There were no more time-saving inventions, whatever for? No more philosophical speculations, meaning had lost its meaning; those who in the past might have given pursuit had instead given themselves over to the anonymity of Verity. There was no political polarity. No medical research. No scientific investigation, not even to probe into a space to escape.

By the year 2008, the Verities were soundly asleep in the past. The Willabies were stupefied within the present; they had stanched the flow of time in an effort to keep it from spilling out: a stasis of tomorrow.

The world was at peace for the first time in millenia.

For many years nothing whatsoever had been heard from Erik Scorbic. Bundi, who by now had thoroughly established his divine dogma, was relieved; it would have been embarrassing to have to remember The Veriest as flesh and blood and bile and phlegm. The Willabies stared into the one-dimensional present without even a blink of peripheral perspective in which to recall "the prognosticator" at all.

When Erik was fourteen his mother, in desperation, fabricated an oracle and let it loose: "The little bird augurs the song of the worm." However, after a brief flutter, this homily failed to fly; instead it swooned in the already miasma of stagnation and fell flat on its too-pointed face.

So that, when Erik was sixteen and almost a man with his broad stooped shoulders and his drooping moustache, nobody gave heed to his warning that, "If the top is ever allowed to stop it will not topple, but reverse its spin." Two months later no one even bothered to listen when Erik declared: "The hiatus is at the end of the inhalation."

By the time Erik came to manhood there were whole cities overgrown with weeds, whole industrial complexes crumbling away, whole networks of electric and telephone wires unravelling. Herds of sheep and cows roamed deserted streets and roving packs of poodles preyed on wild chickens.

It was in the dockweed jungle of what used to be Baltimore that Erik met Alicia — that is what he called her in his mind, it just came to him that that must be her name although he was never to know for sure.

She, like he, was gathering snails after the rain.

She smiled at him, one tooth missing, and proffered her basket so that he could see how many, nearly half full! He looked, and with a flashflood grin he shared with her the secret of his bucket — only four. Alicia laughed, soundlessly.

For awhile they hunted together. She was much quicker to spot them, defter at collecting. Occasionally, when she found a very small one, she would pop it into her mouth shell and all. She did not offer any to Erik, for which he was gratified, not only because he didn't want them but more so because in it was her obvious assumption that he was quite capable of taking care of his own needs.

Eventually, however, she did offer him herself, lifting up her ragged skirt to show her yellow tuft.

From then on, Erik went to be with Alicia nearly every day. She would not come to him, nor go anywhere with him outside her own neighborhood — not even when he brought her a silver comb with which to unsnarl her matted hair. She lived alone in a precarious stone mansion, with no friends other than a brindle mutt.

After several months Erik came to understand that Alicia was pregnant. Although he had never before seen an expectant human mother, he had often watched cats unload their burden of kittens and, once, a goat giving birth to twin kids. Now he kept watch over Alicia, and a gentle pride grew in him, making his passion swell.

It was Anna who betrayed them, Old Anna who followed Erik one day and saw them together in the tall grasses. She screamed and screamed.

The naked Alicia disentangled herself from Erik's embrace and ran at Anna with a sickle. Erik caught her just in time. Wrapping protective arms around her, he pressed her billowy belly to him and smiled into her eyes.

Anna hobbled away, sobbing.

By the next day, however, Anna had recomposed herself within the power of the knowledge that she was to be the grandmother of the first child of the twenty-first century. She called a press conference and told the world.

Pandora's box — so carefully restocked over the past two decades — blew to bits. Amidst the debris, Alicia was captured and confined to an institution where her every move was monitored, channel 42.

Erik was also incarcerated — in a brothel. Where teams of clinicians milked him four times a day and rushed his semen to hospitals around the globe. There it was injected into the eager ovaries of millions of women, many of them old enough to be Erik's grandmother.

All the world watched as Alicia gave birth to her monster. Not until the mother smiled and stretched out her arms to receive the three-eyed infant did the audience release its collective breath in a sigh of acceptance.

The evening of the night that Erik slipped out of the whorehouse window and away forever, he was heard to admonish Cinderella Smith, "How to dance in darkest night: rub your toes with the blood of a bat."

BUD
by
Ian Watson

T plus 300 days. The deep space probe's interior is rather cramped on account of the exercise equipment and the massive shielding against Jupiter's radiation belts. Portholes are all masked at present. Across one viewscreen bulges giant Jupiter itself. The other screens show numbers of the many alien vessels gathered here, some as large as minor moons.

The astronaut glances round his den. He has papered any free space with smuggled centrefolds. Too late to take them down now; besides, he couldn't bear to.

A camera eye watches him, hooked to the two-way video communicating with the nearest alien vessel. He sighs. He presses the call key. The screen snows with static, which resolves into an amorphous, bulging shape. It extrudes something like an eye upon a stalk and bats a hastily convened eyelid at him.

"Bud?"

"What is it, Sexy? We're busy."

"I wish you wouldn't call me that."

"You called me, we didn't call you. So what's

wrong with the name? The Sexies of Earth. What a planet! Do you wish me to call you Earthman? How banal. Lots of beings live on some Earth or other."

"It isn't as though you find us attractive. That's obvious enough. I mean, maybe you'd care about what's going to happen to us if you did. It's just so . . . teasing. Here am I cooped up in a space capsule months from home, months from any human contact."

"You've got your pin-ups."

"Damn it, Bud, everybody on Earth is listening in."

"So I'll shut up. I said we're busy."

"No! Please. Listen, if we're such a funny planet surely we ought to be studied. Preserved, protected — something like that."

"Well, you never know, it might catch on."

"What might?"

"You know what."

"Don't be so damn devious!"

"I thought you wanted me to be more discreet?"

"You're impossible!"

"We think you're pretty improbable yourselves. *Lusus naturae*: a joke of nature. Anyhow, some of you ought to survive. Should be a good test of your reproductive abilities."

"You could evacuate a few million of us. You've got ships and ships out here."

"I told you, we're busy."

"Okay, I realize this is a kind of religious thing with you —"

"Which makes you rather an irreligious thing,

right? A whole planet of snails and sparrows and sperm whales and monkeys thrashing around in rut, penetrating each other, laying eggs and babies and things. Right here in this lovely system where the Budworld swims. I may tell you frankly, quite a few of us felt like putting you out of your misery to start with. But we'll let nature take its course."

"Could we go through this in a bit more detail, Bud? According to our biologists asexual reproduction ought to lead to extinction in the long run. How do you get any evolution? Any variations? New species?"

"Extinction, eh? You should talk. It seems to us that sexual reproduction is a sort of perpetual extinction — over any decent span of macrotime. And the obsessions it produces! Really!"

"I oughtn't to have let you scan the capsule."

"I thought you didn't want that mentioned on an open channel? What's the matter? Are you missing it?"

"Honestly, it isn't such a big thing, Bud. I can do without."

"Oh? Then why do you have your religious images plastered on the walls?"

"Those aren't religious images, they're . . . Oh, never mind."

"Whatever a being takes deep in space with him *is* a religious image."

"I wish they'd sent a woman. If we'd known all this was going to happen —"

"A woman? For you? So you could have spent your time in rut, *doing that,* out here right up close to the Budworld? That would have brought swift retribution."

"No, a woman by herself. A female pilot. They're not so interested in, well, I mean, they don't look at things the same way."

"Don't look at pin-ups? I had the impression that their lives were even more wrapped up in sexual being. Or being sexual."

"Surely we've got a right to our own way of doing things? That's how we all evolved. Blame nature, not us."

"*Lusus naturae.* The exception proves the rule."

"You're well up on the folk wisdom today."

"My job, Sexy. To keep you out of our hair, while we get on with the real business — of witness. We're quite charitable, you know. This is just latrine duty for me. I pulled it for a spot of insubordination to the Chief Bud."

"You've become very idiomatic, if you're not all that interested."

"Think nothing of it. Your troubles will soon be over."

"They aren't troubles!"

"Can you honestly say that?"

"Sure, we have problems. Deer do, rats do, gorillas do, spiders do, we all do."

"How much time you all waste on it! No wonder you've got nowhere in the universe after millions of years. Changing your species every five minutes. Even your present civilization is all sublimation, according to your priest Freud."

"We oughtn't to have beamed you so much data."

"Then we'd have had nothing to talk about. I suppose it's my own perversity that makes me bother — as witnessed by insubordination to the Chief Bud."

"Think you're pretty clever, don't you?"

"Sexy, I'm four point three billion years old, bud by bud to the Nth. How long do you lot live? Oh, forget it!"

"In all that time you ought to have accumulated a bit of wisdom and compassion. That's the trouble with you. You're much the same as you were back in the beginning. You don't evolve."

"We spread, friend. We spread. And all the other species in the Pancivic are budders — using the term species loosely. It's the way. Listen, life in the universe is this way: and I'll only tell you once more. The whole universe is alive. It's one huge living thing: galaxies, stars, worlds, the lot. You just live too short a time to notice the rhythms of this life. And one of these rhythms is the flow of our sort of life over worlds and between them. Every single atom in the universe senses the cosmic flow, so that life comes together — gets it together — by a simple clumping of most any kind of matter: a conglomeration. As soon as there's a clumping, the cosmic mind-field flows into the clump, splits into it; and that life clumps bigger, so you get an organised being — mentally organised, but it doesn't need any specific shape. Any shape'll do. Any shape'll become any other shape. We're all amorphous. We don't spend our time trying on different suits of clothes for millions of years on end and having to wear them willy-nilly even if the sleeves are too damn long or the boots are too heavy to pick up. We choose whatever form we like. And life spreads itself around by splitting, growing, splitting and so on. It's a simple universe, and this is the way things are in it. Life's simple too. You're the most perversely, complicated, damaged things we've ever come across. A perpetual one-off experiment. You'd think the universe was a complicated place, the way you're set up."

"Perhaps it's more complicated than you think, Bud. Perhaps we can see that and you can't. Perhaps we've evolved to grasp that knowledge."

"Perhaps pigs have wings."

"So you could be a winged pig if you wanted to?"

"Right. A new form, for the hell of it. Whereas you'd have to spend half a million years chasing pigs over fences or mating them with buzzards to arrive at that sublime foolishness, and be locked in it. Life multi-adapts *at will. Real* life does. Some of us don't think you're really alive at all. You're a sort of world-wide construction set for building ridiculous specialised machines. Perhaps some bud fixed your place up as a joke or a playground. Everything's so incompatible with everything else. Unstable situation! We never expected to find you messing around in space."

"Never expected? Do you mean you've visited Earth before?"

"No, the Budworld. We were here for the last budding — oh, what, about three millenia ago? When you got your second planet budded out — the hot white one."

"Venus."

"Sure, when Venus budded out of the Budworld. That's how little worlds get born."

"Which is what the Great Red Spot is. A new world."

"You do need telling a lot of times."

"But there's no room for any more planets near

the sun. Gravitational inhibition — it's a law of physics.''

"You made the law, so you tell the Budworld that. It's Budworld's family after all. Oh, there'll be room. A bit of elbowing around and they'll all fit in. You'll see — or maybe not. Maybe Mercury will become a moon of the new one.''

"What about the Earth, for Chrissake? What about our home?''

"Oh, it'll fit in too. A bit nearer the sun, a bit further out. Maybe it'll even get detached and go a-wandering. Leave home, as it were. Planets do.''

"Frozen solid. No air. No seas.''

"Now, if you were *real* life you could adapt to that. Shape-shift. Become frost-giants or ice-beasts. But the way you're set up it would take a million years. You know, this sort of thing's going on all the time — planets birthing and bumping each other over, novae and supernovae, stars diving into dust clouds. Speed the universe up, and it's a wow. Real life has to put up with *that*. You've been living a sheltered life down here.''

"So how long have we got?''

"We reckon the Red Spot's due to bud out any day now. It'll take, oh, a year or so for the new world to slide down the gravity gradient sunwards to find its place. We'll stick around to see where it ends up.''

"But is it definitely going to hit us, Bud?''

"Hit you? No. Not *exactly*. It'll have built up a lot of repulsion charge. It'll just cannon off you, still some way out. Probably flip your world over. North-South reversal: change of night sky when the murk clears. Push your world into a new orbit. That sort of thing. It can't miss you entirely, if that's what you're hoping. Major planets are all lined up this year. Auspicious birth, eh?"

"What can we *do*? As a friend, *please* —"

"That's up to you. What I'd suggest is, if you've only got one card in your hand you'd better play it and keep on playing it, even if it is a joker."

"What kind of suggestion is that?"

"I guess you'd call it a Saturnalia. Only you got the name wrong . . . Better to call it a Jovenalia. Or a Budworldia."

"It sounds more like a can of beer."

"That could help out, too."

T plus 750 days. He still thinks in Mission time, though he splashed down three months ago. Since then, he has enjoyed the favors of many young ladies, which he feels is only his due. Here is one more of them, in his hotel room. She has red hair.

"What did they look like, honey? You're the only man who ever got close to them."

"I was just in a parking orbit. Not all that close to them. Hell, I don't know what they looked like. Anything and everything. Blobs. Pretty shapeless."

"At least you're in shape. Considering all the zero-gee. You did the exercises."

"And you're . . . Hey, do that again."

"Feel good?"

"Mmm."

"Doesn't it make you feel sort of good that we can do something they can't? Well? Doesn't it make you feel kind of proud? I wonder, are all the rabbits and whales and butterflies and ostriches and frogs in the world up to it too, right now? I guess it must be a pretty flat existence for those blobs, considering. I mean, who likes splitting in half?"

"Who indeed? We'll show them."

By now, the mass that has split from Jupiter — the erstwhile Great Red Spot — is larger than the Moon itself, outside the window. Incandescent, it lights up the whole night sky and the city. In the bedroom their bodies are lit up too.

Survival reaction, he thinks in a detached moment; then he forgets about thinking.

All over the Earth, billions of creatures are enjoying themselves. And each other. Furiously.

THE MAKING OF
REVELATION, *PART I*
by
Philip José Farmer

God said, "Bring me Cecil B. DeMille."

"Dead or alive?" the angel Gabriel said.

"I want to make him an offer he can't refuse. Can even *I* do this to a dead man?"

"Oh, I see," said Gabriel, who didn't. "It will be done."

And it was.

Cecil Blount DeMille, confused, stood in front of the desk. He didn't like it. He was used to sitting behind the desk while others stood. Considering the circumstances, he wasn't about to protest. The giant, divinely handsome, bearded, pipe-smoking man behind the desk was not one you'd screw around with. However, the gray eyes, though steely, weren't quite those of a Wall Street banker. They held a hint of compassion.

Unable to meet those eyes, DeMille looked at the angel by his side. He'd always thought angels had wings. This one didn't, though he could certainly fly. He'd carried DeMille in his arms up

through the stratosphere to a city of gold somewhere between the Earth and the moon. Without
a space suit, too.

God, like all great entities, came right to the
point.

"This is 1980 A.D. In twenty years it'll be time
for The Millennium. The day of judgement. The
events as depicted in the Book of Revelation or
the Apocalypse by St. John the Divine. You know,
the seven seals, the four horsemen, the moon
dripping blood, Armageddon, and all that."

DeMille wished he'd be invited to sit down.
Being dead for twenty-one years, during which
he'd not moved a muscle, had tended to weaken
him.

"Take a chair," God said. "Gabe, bring the man
a brandy." He puffed on his pipe; tiny lightning
crackled through the clouds of smoke.

"Here you are, Mr. DeMille," Gabriel said,
handing him the liqueur in a cut quartz goblet.
"Napoleon 1880."

DeMille knew there wasn't any such thing as
a one-hundred year old brandy, but he didn't argue. Anyway, the stuff certainly tasted like it was.
They really lived up here.

God sighed, and he said, "The main trouble is
that not many people really believe in Me any
more. So My powers are not what they once were.
The old gods, Zeus, Odin, all that bunch, lost
their strength and just faded away, like old soldiers, when their worshippers ceased to believe
in them.

"So, I just can't handle the end of the world by
Myself any more. I need someone with experi-

ence, know-how, connections, and a reputation. Somebody people know really existed. You. Unless you know of somebody who's made more Biblical epics than you have."

"That'll be the day," DeMille said. "But what about the unions? They really gave me a hard time, the commie bas . . . uh, so-and-so's. Are they as strong as ever?"

"You wouldn't believe their clout nowadays."

DeMille bit his lip, then said, "I want them dissolved. If I only got twenty years to produce this film, I can't be held up by a bunch of goldbrickers."

"No way," God said. "They'd all strike, and we can't afford any delays."

He looked at his big railroad watch. "We're going to be on a very tight schedule."

"Well, I don't know," DeMille said. "You can't get anything done with all their regulations, interunion jealousies, and the featherbedding. And the wages! It's no wonder it's so hard to show a profit. It's too much of a hassle!"

"I can always get D. W. Griffith."

DeMille's face turned red. "You want a grade-B production? No, no, that's all right! I'll do it, do it!"

God smiled and leaned back. "I thought so. By the way, you're not the producer, too; I am. My angels will be the executive producers. They haven't had much to do for several millennia, and the devil makes work for idle hands, you know. Haw, haw! You'll be the chief director, of course. But this is going to be quite a job. You'll have to have at least a hundred thousand assistant directors."

"But . . . that means training about 99,000 directors!"

"That's the least of our problems. Now you can see why I want to get things going immediately."

DeMille gripped the arms of the chair and said, weakly, "Who's going to finance this?"

God frowned. "That's another problem. My Antagonist has control of all the banks. If worse comes to worse, I could melt down the heavenly city and sell it. But the bottom of the gold market would drop all the way to hell. And I'd have to move to Beverly Hills. You wouldn't believe the smog there or the prices they're asking for houses.

"However, I think I can get the money. Leave that to Me."

The men who really owned the American banks sat at a long mahogany table in a huge room in a Manhattan skyscraper. The Chairman of the Board sat at the head. He didn't have the horns, tail, and hooves which legend gave him. Nor did he have an odor of brimstone. More like Brut. He was devilishly handsome and the biggest and best-built man in the room. He looked like he could have been the chief of the angels and in fact once had been. His eyes *were* evil but no more so than the others at the table, bar one.

The exception, Raphael, sat at the other end of the table. The only detractions from his angelic appearance were his bloodshot eyes. His apartment on the West Side had paper-thin walls, and the swingers' party next door had kept him awake most of the night. Despite his fatigue, he'd been quite effective in presenting the offer from above.

Don Francisco "The Fixer" Fica drank a sixth

glass of wine to up his courage, made the sign of the cross, most offensive to the Chairman, gulped, and spoke.

"I'm sorry, Signor, but that's the way the vote went. One hundred percent. It's a purely business proposition, legal, too, and there's no way we won't make a huge profit from it. We're gonna finance the movie, come hell or high water!"

Satan reared up from his chair and slammed a huge but well-manicured fist onto the table. Glasses of vino crashed over; plates half-filled with pasta and spaghetti rattled. All but Raphael paled.

"*Dio motarello! Lecaculi! Cacasotti! Non romperci i coglioni!* I'm the Chairman, and I say no, no, no!"

Fica looked at the other heads of the families. Mignotta, Fregna, Stronza, Loffa, Recchione, and Bocchino seemed scared, but each nodded the go-ahead at Fica.

"I'm indeed sorry that you don't see it our way," Fica said. "But I must ask for your resignation."

Only Raphael could meet The Big One's eyes, but business was business. Satan cursed and threatened. Nevertheless, he was stripped of all his shares of stock. He'd walked in the richest man in the world, and he stormed out penniless and an ex-member of the Organization.

Raphael caught up with him as he strode mumbling up Park Avenue.

"You're the father of lies," Raphael said, "so you can easily be a great success as an actor or politician. There's money in both fields. Fame, too. I suggest acting. You've got more friends in Hollywood than anywhere else."

"Are you nuts?" Satan snarled.

"No. Listen. I'm authorized to sign you up for the film on the end of the world. You'll be a lead, get top billing. You'll have to share it with The Son, but we can guarantee you a bigger dressing room than His. You'll be playing yourself, so it ought to be easy work."

Satan laughed so loudly that he cleared the sidewalks for two blocks. The Empire State Building swayed more than it should have in the wind.

"You and your boss must think I'm pretty dumb! Without me the film's a flop. You're up a creek without a paddle. Why should I help you? If I do I end up at the bottom of a flaming pit forever. Bug off!"

Raphael shouted after him, "We can always get Roman Polanski!"

Raphael reported to God, who was taking His ease on His jasper and cornelian throne above which glowed a rainbow.

"He's right, Your Divinity. If he refuses to cooperate, the whole deal's off. No real Satan, no real Apocalypse."

God smiled. "We'll see."

Raphael wanted to ask Him what He had in mind. But an angel appeared with a request that God come to the special effects department. Its technicians were having trouble with the roll-up-the-sky-like-a-scroll machine.

"Schmucks!" God growled. "Do I have to do everything?"

Satan moved into a tenement on 121st Street and went on welfare. It wasn't a bad life, not for one who was used to Hell. But two months later, his checks quit coming. There was no unemployment any more. Anyone who was capable of working but wouldn't was out of luck. What had happened was that Central Casting had hired everybody in the world as production workers, stars, bit players, or extras.

Meanwhile, all the advertising agencies in the world had spread the word, good or bad depending upon the viewpoint, that the Bible was true. If you weren't a Christian, and, what was worse, a sincere Christian, you were doomed to perdition.

Raphael shot up to Heaven again.

"My God, You wouldn't believe what's happening! The Christians are repenting of their sins and promising to be good forever and ever, amen! The Jews, Moslems, Hindus, Buddhists, scientologists, animists, you name them, are lining up at the baptismal fonts! What a mess! The atheists have converted, too, and all the communist and Marxian socialist governments have been overthrown!"

"That's nice," God said. "But I'll really believe in the sincerity of the Christian nations when they kick out their present administrations. Down to the local dogcatcher."

"They're doing it!" Raphael shouted. "But maybe You don't understand! This isn't the way things go in the *Book of Revelation!* We'll have to do some very extensive rewriting of the script! Unless You straighten things out!"

God seemed very calm. "The script? How's Ellison coming along with it?"

Of course, God knew everything that was happening, but He pretended sometimes that He didn't. It was His excuse for talking. Just issuing a command every once in a while made for long silences, sometimes lasting for centuries.

He had hired only science-fiction writers to work on the script since they were the only ones with imaginations big enough to handle the job. Besides, they weren't bothered by scientific impossibilities. God loved Ellison, the head writer, because he was the only human he'd met so far who wasn't afraid to argue with Him. Ellison was severely handicapped, however, because he wasn't allowed to use obscenities while in His presence.

"Ellison's going to have a hemorrhage when he finds out about the rewrites," Raphael said. "He gets screaming mad if anyone messes around with his scripts."

"I'll have him up for dinner," God said. "If he gets too obstreperous, I'll toss around a few lightning bolts. If he thinks he was burned before . . . Well!"

Raphael wanted to question God about the tampering with the book, but just then the head of Budgets came in. The angel beat it. God got very upset when He had to deal with money matters.

The head assistant director said, "We got a big problem now, Mr. DeMille. We can't have any Armageddon. Israel's willing to rent the site to us, but where are we going to get the forces of Gog and Magog to fight against the good guys? Everybody's converted. Nobody's willing to fight on the side of anti-Christ and Satan. That means we've got to change the script again. I don't want to be the one to tell Ellison . . ."

"Do I have to think of everything?" DeMille said. "It's no problem. Just hire actors to play the villains."

"I already thought of that. But they want a bonus. They say they might be persecuted just for playing the guys in the black hats. They call it the social-stigma bonus. But the guilds and the unions won't go for it. Equal pay for all extras or no movie and that's that."

DeMille sighed. "It won't make any difference anyway as long as we can't get Satan to play himself."

The assistant nodded. So far, they'd been shooting around the devil's scenes. But they couldn't put it off much longer.

DeMille stood up. "I have to watch the auditions for The Great Whore of Babylon."

The field of 100,000 candidates for the role had been narrowed to a hundred, but from what he'd heard none of these could play the part. They were all good Christians now, no matter what they'd been before, and they just didn't have their hearts in the role. DeMille had intended to cast his brand-new mistress, a starlet, a hot little number — if promises meant anything — one hundred percent right for the part. But just before they went to bed for the first time, he'd gotten a phone call.

"None of this hankypanky, C.B.," God had said. "You're now a devout worshipper of Me, one of the lost sheep that's found its way back to the fold. So get with it. Otherwise, back to Forest Lawn for you, and I use Griffith."

"But . . . but I'm Cecil B. DeMille! The rules are O.K. for the common people, but . . ."

"Throw that scarlet woman out! Shape up or ship out! If you marry her, fine! But remember, there'll be no more divorces!"

DeMille was glum. Eternity was going to be like living forever next door to the Board of Censors.

The next day, his secretary, very excited, buzzed him.

"Mr. DeMille! Satan's here! I don't have him for an appointment, but he says he's always had a long-standing one with you!"

Demoniac laughter bellowed through the intercom.

"C.B., my boy! I've changed my mind! I tried out anonymously for the part, but your shithead assistant said I wasn't the type for the role! So I've come to you! I can start work as soon as we sign the contract!"

The contract, however, was not the one the great director had in mind. Satan, smoking a big cigar, chuckling, cavorting, read the terms.

"And don't worry about signing in your blood. It's unsanitary. Just ink in your John Henry, and all's well that ends in Hell."

"You get my soul," DeMille said weakly.

"It's not much of a bargain for me. But if you don't sign it, you won't get me. Without me, the movie's a bomb. Ask The Producer, He'll tell you how it is."

"I'll call Him now."

"No! Sign now, this very second, or I walk out forever!"

DeMille bowed his head, more in pain than in prayer.

"Now!"

DeMille wrote on the dotted line. There had

never been any genuine indecision. After all, he
was a film director.

After snickering Satan had left, DeMille punched
a phone number. The circuits transmitted this to
a station which beamed the pulses up to a satellite which transmitted these directly to the
heavenly city. Somehow, he got a wrong number.
He hung up quickly when Israfel, the angel of
death, answered. The second attempt, he got
through.

"Your Divinity, I suppose You know what I
just did? It *was* the only way we could get him
to play himself. You understand that, don't
You?"

"Yes, but if you're thinking of breaking the contract or getting Me to do it for you, forget it. What
kind of an image would I have if I did something
unethical like that? But not to worry. He can't get
his hooks into your soul until I say so."

Not to worry? DeMille thought. I'm the one
who's going to Hell, not Him.

"Speaking of hooks, let Me remind you of a
clause in your contract with The Studio. If you
ever fall from grace, and I'm not talking about
that little bimbo you were going to make your
mistress, you'll die. The Mafia isn't the only one
that puts out a contract. *Capice?*"

DeMille, sweating and cold, hung up. In a
sense, he was already in Hell. All his life with
no women except for one wife? It was bad enough
to have no variety, but what if whoever he married cut him off, like one of his wives — what
was her name? — had done?

Moreover, he couldn't get loaded out of his
skull even to forget his marital woes. God, though

not prohibiting booze in His Book, had said that moderation in strong liquor was required and no excuses. Well, maybe he could drink beer, however disgustingly plebeian that was.

He wasn't even happy with his work now. He just didn't get the respect he had in the old days. When he chewed out the camerapeople, the grips, the gaffers, the actors, they stormed back at him that he didn't have the proper Christian humility, he was too high and mighty, too arrogant. God would get him if he didn't watch his big fucking mouth.

This left him speechless and quivering. He'd always thought, and acted accordingly, that the director, not God, was God. He remembered telling Charlton Heston that when Heston, who after all was only Moses, had thrown a temper tantrum when he'd stepped in a pile of camel shit during the filming of *The Ten Commandments*.

Was there more to the making of the end-of-the-world than appeared on the surface? Had God seemingly forgiven everybody their sins and lack of faith but was subtly, even insidiously, making everybody pay by suffering? Had He forgiven but not forgotten? Or vice versa?

God marked even the fall of a sparrow, though why the sparrow, a notoriously obnoxious and dirty bird, should be significant in God's eye was beyond DeMille.

He had the uneasy feeling that everything wasn't as simple and as obvious as he'd thought when he'd been untimely ripped from the grave in a sort of Caesarean section and carried off like a nursing baby in Gabriel's arms to the office of The Ultimate Producer.

From the *Playboy* Interview feature, December, 1990.

Playboy: Mr. Satan, why did you decide to play yourself after all?

Satan: Damned if I know.

Playboy: The rumors are that you'll be required to wear clothes in the latter-day scenes but that you steadfastly refuse. Are these rumors true?

Satan: Yes indeed. Everybody knows I never wear clothes except when I want to appear among humans without attracting undue attention. If I wear clothes it'd be unrealistic. It'd be phoney, though God knows there are enough fake things in this movie. The Producer says this is going to be a PG picture, not an X-rated. That's why I walked off the set the other day. My lawyers are negotiating with The Studio now about this. But you can bet your ass that I won't go back unless things go my way, the right way. After all, I am an artist, and I have my integrity. Tell me, if you had a prong this size, would you hide it?

Playboy: The Chicago cops would arrest me before I got a block from my pad. I don't know, though, if they'd charge me with indecent exposure or being careless with a natural resource.

Satan: They wouldn't dare arrest me. I got too much on the city administration.

Playboy: That's some whopper. But I thought angels were sexless. You are a fallen angel, aren't you?

Satan: You jerk! What kind of researcher are you? Right there in the Bible, Genesis 6:2, it says that the sons of God, that is, the angels, took the daughters of men as wives and had children by them. You think the kids were test tube babies?

Also, you dunce, I refer you to Jude 7 where it's said that the angels, like the Sodomites, committed fornications and followed unnatural lusts.

Playboy: Whew! That brimstone! There's no need getting so hot under the collar, Mr. Satan. I only converted a few years ago. I haven't had much chance to read the Bible.

Satan: I read the Bible every day. All of it. I'm a speedreader, you know.

Playboy: You read the Bible? (Pause). Hee, hee! Do you read it for the same reason W. C. Fields did when he was dying?

Satan: What's that?

Playboy: Looking for loopholes.

DeMille was in a satellite and supervising the camerapeople while they shot the takes from ten miles up. He didn't like at all the terrific pressure he was working under. There was no chance to shoot every scene three or four times to get the best angle. Or to reshoot if the actors blew their lines. And, oh, sweet Jesus, they were blowing them all over the world!

He mopped his bald head. "I don't care what The Producer says! We have to retake at least a thousand scenes. And we've a million miles of film to go yet!"

They were getting close to the end of the breaking-of-the-seven-seals sequences. The Lamb, played by The Producer's Son, had just broken the sixth seal. The violent worldwide earthquake had gone well. The sun-turning-black-as-a-funeral-pall had been a breeze. But the moon-all-red-as-blood had had some color problems. The rushes looked more like Colonel Sanders' orange juice than hemoglobin. In DeMille's opinion the stars-falling-to-earth-like-figs-shaken-down-by-a-gale scenes had been excellent, visually speaking. But everybody knew that the stars were not little blazing stones set in the sky but were colossal balls of atomic fires each of which was many times bigger than Earth. Even one of them, a million miles from Earth, would destroy it. So where was the credibility factor?

"I don't understand you, boss," DeMille's assistant said. "You didn't worry about credibility when you made *The Ten Commandments*. When Heston, I mean, Moses, parted the Red Sea, it was the fakiest thing I ever saw. It must've made unbelievers out of millions of Christians. But the film was a box-office success."

"It was the dancing girls that brought off the whole thing!" DeMille screamed. "Who cares about all that other bullshit when they can see all those beautiful long-legged snatches twirling their veils!"

His secretary floated from her chair. "I quit, you male chauvinistic pig! So me and my sisters are just snatches to you, you bald-headed cunt?"

His hotline to the heavenly city rang. He picked up the phone.

"Watch your language!" The Producer thundered. "If you step out of line too many times, I'll send you back to the grave! And Satan gets you right then and there!"

Chastened but boiling near the danger point, DeMille got back to business, called Art in Hollywood. The sweep of the satellite around Earth included the sky-vanishing-as-a-scroll-is-rolled-up scenes, where every-mountain-and-island-is-removed-from-its-place. If the script had called for a literal removing, the tectonics problem would have been terrific and perhaps impossible. But in this case the special effects departments only had to simulate the scenes.

Even so, the budget was strained. However, The Producer, through his unique abilities, was able to carry these off. Whereas, in the original script, genuine displacements of Greenland, England, Ireland, Japan, and Madagascar had been called for, not to mention thousands of smaller islands, these were only faked.

"Your Divinity, I have some bad news," Raphael said.

The Producer was too busy to indulge in talking about something He already knew. Millions of the faithful had backslid and taken up their old sinful ways. They believed that since so many events of the apocalypse were being faked, God must not be capable of making any really big catastrophes. So, they didn't have anything to worry about.

The Producer, however, had decided that it would not only be good to wipe out some of the wicked but it would strengthen the faithful if they saw that God still had some muscle.

"They'll get the real thing next time," He said. "But we have to give DeMille time to set up his cameras at the right places. And we'll have to have the script rewritten, of course."

Raphael groaned. "Couldn't somebody else tell Ellison? He'll carry on something awful."

"I'll tell him. You look pretty pooped, Rafe. You need a little R&R. Take two weeks off. But don't do it on Earth. Things are going to be very unsettling there for a while."

Raphael, who had a tender heart, said, "Thanks, Boss. I'd just as soon not be around to see it."

The seal was stamped on the foreheads of the faithful, marking them safe from the burning of a third of Earth, the turning of a third of the sea to blood along with the sinking of a third of the ships at sea (which also included the crashing of a third of the airplanes in the air, something St. John had overlooked), the turning of a third of all water to wormwood (a superfluous measure since a third was already thoroughly polluted), the failure of a third of daylight, the release of giant mutant locusts from the abyss, and the release of poison-gas-breathing mutant horses, which slew a third of mankind.

DeMille was delighted. Never had such terrifying scenes been filmed. And these were nothing to the plagues which followed. He had enough film from the cutting room to make a hundred documentaries after the movie was shown. And then he got a call from The Producer.

"It's back to the special effects, my boy."

"But why, Your Divinity? We still have to shoot the-Great-Whore-of-Babylon sequences, the two-Beasts-and-the-marking-of-the-wicked, the Mount-Zion-and-The-Lamb-with-His-one-hundred-and-forty-thousand-good-men-who-haven't-defiled-themselves-with-women, the . . ."

"Because there aren't any wicked left by now, you dolt! And not too many of the good, either!"

"That couldn't be helped," DeMille said. "Those gas-breathing, scorpion-tailed horses kind of got out of hand. But we just *have* to have the scenes where the rest of mankind that survives the plagues still doesn't abjure its worship of idols and doesn't repent of its murders, sorcery, fornications, and robberies."

"Rewrite the script."

"Ellison will quit for sure this time."

"That's all right. I already have some hack from Peoria lined up to take his place. And cheaper, too."

DeMille took his outfit, one hundred thousand strong, to the heavenly city. Here they shot the war between Satan and his demons and Michael and his angels. This was not in the chronological sequence as written by St. John. But the logistics problems were so tremendous that it was thought best to film these out of order.

Per the rewritten script, Satan and his host were defeated, but a lot of nonbelligerents were casualties, including DeMille's best cameraperson. Moreover, there was a delay in production when Satan insisted that a stuntperson do the part where he was hurled from heaven to Earth.

"Or use a dummy!" he yelled. "Twenty thousand miles is a hell of a long way to fall! If I'm hurt badly I might not be able to finish the movie!"

The screaming match between the director and Satan took place on the edge of the city. The Producer, unnoticed, came up behind Satan and kicked him from the city for the second time in their relationship with utter ruin and furious combustion.

Shrieking, "I'll sue! I'll sue!" Satan fell towards the planet below. He made a fine spectacle in his blazing entrance into the atmosphere, but the people on Earth paid it little attention. They were used to fiery portents in the sky. In fact, they were getting fed up with them.

DeMille screamed and danced around and jumped up and down. Only the presence of The Producer kept him from using foul and abusive language.

"We didn't get it on camera! Now we'll have to shoot it over!"

"His contract calls for only one fall," God said. "You'd better shoot the War-between-The-Faithful - and - True - Rider - against - the - beast - and - the - false-prophet while he recovers."

"What'll I do about the fall?" DeMille moaned.

"Fake it," The Producer said, and He went back to His office.

Per the script, an angel came down from heaven and bound up the badly injured and burned and groaning Satan with a chain and threw him into the abyss, the Grand Canyon. Then he shut and sealed it over him (what a terrific sequence that was!) so that Satan might seduce the nations no more until a thousand years had passed.

A few years later the devil's writhings caused a volcano to form above him, and the Environmental Protection Agency filed suit against Celestial Productions, Inc. because of the resultant pollution of the atmosphere.

Then God, very powerful now that only believers existed on Earth, performed the first resurrection. In this, only the martyrs were raised. And Earth, which had had much elbow room because of the recent wars and plagues, was suddenly crowded again.

Part I was finished except for the reshooting of some scenes, the dubbing in of voice and background noise, and the synchronization of the music, which was done by the cherubim and seraphim (all now unionized).

The great night of the premiere in a newly built theater in Hollywood, six million capacity, arrived. DeMille got a standing ovation after it was over. But *Time* and *Newsweek* and *The Manchester Guardian* panned the movie.

"There are some people who may go to hell after all," God growled.

DeMille didn't care about that. The film was a box-office success, grossing ten billion dollars in the first six months. And when he considered the reruns in theaters and the TV rights . . . well, had anyone ever done better?

He had a thousand more years to live. That seemed like a long time. Now. But . . . what would happen to him when Satan was released to seduce the nations again? According to John the Divine's book, there'd be another worldwide battle. Then Satan, defeated, would be cast into the lake of fire and sulphur in the abyss.

(He'd be allowed to keep his Oscar, however.)

Would God let Satan, per the contract DeMille had signed with the devil, take DeMille with him into the abyss? Or would He keep him safe long enough to finish directing Part II? After Satan was buried for good, there'd be a second resurrection and a judging of those raised from the dead. The goats, the bad guys, would be hurled into the pit to keep Satan company. DeMille should be with the saved, the sheep, because he had been born again. But there was that contract with The Tempter.

DeMille arranged a conference with The Producer. Ostensibly, it was about Part II, but DeMille managed to bring up the subject which really interested him.

"I can't break your contract with him," God said.

"But I only signed it so that You'd be sure to get Satan for the role. It was a self-sacrifice. Greater love hath no man and all that. Doesn't that count for anything?"

"Let's discuss the shooting of the new heaven and the new earth sequences."

At least I'm not going to be put into hell until the movie is done, DeMille thought. But after that? He couldn't endure thinking about it.

"It's going to be a terrible technical problem," God said, interrupting DeMille's gloomy thoughts. "When the second resurrection takes place, there won't be even Standing Room Only on Earth. That's why I'm dissolving the old earth and making a new one. But I can't just duplicate the old Earth. The problem of Lebensraum would still remain. Now, what I'm contemplating is a Dyson sphere."

"What's that?"

"A scheme by a 20th-century mathematician to break up the giant planet Jupiter into large pieces and set them in orbit at the distance of Earth from the sun. The surfaces of the pieces would provide room for a population enormously larger than Earth's. It's a Godlike concept."

"What a documentary its filming would be!" DeMille said. "Of course, if we could write some love interest in it, we could make a he . . . pardon me, a heaven of a good story!"

God looked at his big railroad watch.

"I have another appointment, C.B. The conference is over."

DeMille said goodby and walked dejectedly towards the door. He still hadn't gotten an answer about his ultimate fate. God was stringing him along. He felt that he wouldn't know until the last minute what was going to happen to him. He'd be suffering a thousand years of uncertainty, of mental torture. His life would be a cliff-hanger. Will God relent? Or will He save the hero at the very last second?

"C.B.," God said.

DeMille spun around, his heart thudding, his knees turned to water. Was this it? The fatal finale? Had God, in His mysterious and subtle way, decided for some reason that there'd be no Continued In Next Chapter for him? It didn't seem likely, but then The Producer had never promised that He'd use him as the director of Part II nor had He signed a contract with him. Maybe, like so many temperamental producers, He'd suddenly concluded that DeMille wasn't the right one for the job. Which meant that He could arrange it so that his ex-director would be thrown now, right this minute, into the lake of fire.

God said, "I can't break your contract with Satan. So . . ."

"Yes?"

DeMille's voice sounded to him as if he were speaking very far away.

"Satan can't have your soul until you die."

"Yes?"

His voice was only a trickle of sound, a last few drops of water from a clogged drainpipe.

"So, if you don't die, and that, of course, depends upon your behavior, Satan can't ever have your soul."

God smiled and said, "See you in eternity."

REBECCA RUBINSTEIN'S SEVENTEENTH BIRTHDAY
by
Simon Gandolfi

The first morning of mid-term break most of her school friends would sleep late — but not Rebecca Rubinstein. This promised to be the most important day of her life; her seventeenth birthday and Rik Smith was taking her somewhere special.

"For a unique experience," he had told her quietly, "there's no one else I could share it with." Then he had kissed her lingeringly on the lips and her stomach had melted the way it always did when Rik kissed her . . . and as it melted now as she lay in bed just thinking about him.

"Look at you," her mother was forever complaining. "You could be dating any boy in the school and you have to pick on a *schwartze*.

When Rebecca remained silent (which she did once she had learned that there was no answer to her mother's protests — or no answer capable of satisfying her mother), her mother would say,

"That this should happen to me. I mean, *why* Rik Smith?"

Any girl in Rebecca's class could have supplied the answer: Rik Smith was different. And any girl in her class would have given most anything to be dating Rik Smith.

What her mother should be asking, thought Rebecca, is *Why is Rik Smith dating Rebecca Rubinstein?*

Sure, she was beautiful, Rebecca admitted; but not as beautiful as either Susan Schwartz or Helen Katz. Anyway, Rik dated her for her company more than for her looks. This was another way in which he was different from the other boys. It wasn't that he didn't like girls; she could tell he did from the way his lips trembled on hers as they kissed. But he wasn't forever dragging at her clothes and trying to get his hands on her breasts the way Abbie Kaufman had . . . not that Rebecca disliked hands on her breasts, or the idea of hands on her breasts. She would *love* to feel Rik Smith's hands. No, it was how Abbie Kaufman had done it; a sort of way that reminded Rebecca of her father's dog, Plato, and the way Plato got excited over a bone.

Being made to feel like your father's dog's bone wasn't much fun in Rebecca Rubinstein's opinion.

Abbie Kaufman had been her previous boyfriend. Her mother had liked Abbie; his father was President of the board at CCT Mining and CCT was the biggest mining concern in this space section outside of the inter-galactic conglomerates such as RTZ INTERSPACE.

It was Abbie Kaufman who had first drawn

Rebecca's attention to Rik Smith the day Rik transferred to Springland High. Most boys freshly arrived on a planet and joining a new school would have taken care to adapt to local custom, if only in dress. Rik had merely gone his own way and dressed his own way in clothes out of the history books he was forever studying.

"Who does he think he is?" Abbie Kaufman had demanded, "Decked out like that!"

But what Rebecca Rubinstein had noticed was neither Rik's clothes nor even the deep brown of his skin. She had noticed his eyes. They were the darkest and the warmest eyes Rebecca had ever seen, calm eyes . . .

"It's as if he's looking at you from a million miles away," had been Susan Schwartz's comment. "Kind of spooky but nice."

Definitely nice, Rebecca thought as she slipped out of bed and touched the control button. The bedroom walls faded from soft blue into a misty transparency through which she could see the wide lawns stretching away to the shrubbery dividing their garden from the temperate forest. A gray, slab-shaped robot busily snipped at the border of the rosebed beneath her room. It was a new robot. Her father had bought it. The garden was his domain and all the garden robots looked alike. "I prefer my machines unobtrusive," he had protested gently when Rebecca had accused him of lacking fantasy.

Well, Rik wasn't lacking in fantasy, Rebecca thought as she shed her nightdress and turned to face the mirror above her dressing table. *Her seventeenth birthday and a unique experience:* she knew what Rik had meant by that and she had

already decided she would let him. She was
ready. She had been ready from her first date with
Rik Smith the previous semester.

*A unique experience he could only share with
her* . . . what a lovely way of saying it, she thought
and ran her hands over her hips and down her
thighs. Then she nearly screamed. It couldn't be!
Leaning close to the mirror, she gaped at her chin.
The beginnings of a pimple!

Her hands flew amongst the array of tubes and
bottles on the dressing table. Bitter experience
told her that none of the salves and lotions would
do any good. For a moment she considered fling-
ing herself back on her bed and weeping. This
day of all days! How could she surrender her
virginity to Rik Smith with her chin in such a
state?

Close to despair, she grabbed up a robe and
stepped onto the circular elevator pad. The pad
sank down the stem supporting her room and she
ran out to the garden terrace where her parents
were already at breakfast.

Her parents met her with a chorused, "Happy
birthday!"

Happy birthday indeed! "Mama," she wailed,
"Look!"

Her mother looked and was pleased at what
she saw. "You would go out with that Rik
Smith — what sort of food has he been feeding
you?"

Her father, recognizing the opening shots of an
argument, ducked back behind the book he'd
propped against the coffee pot. "I thought he was
coming to fetch you at half past nine," he mumbled at the book. "Shouldn't you get dressed?"

"You!" was all Rebecca found to answer. With a toss of her head, she glared at her parents. "Anyway, he said he was bringing me a special dress he wants me to wear."

"So now the clothes we buy for you aren't good enough," said her mother.

"I never said that."

"You just did."

"Now, mother . . ." her father protested.

"So whose side are you on?" demanded Mrs. Rubinstein — and, to her daughter, "Your birthday and you go off with a stranger. Don't we mean anything to you?"

Right now what they meant to Rebecca was a drag; at least her mother was a drag with her continual attempts at laying guilt. "Why do you have to spoil everything?"

"It wasn't my food that gave you that spot."

Her father humphed his relief at spotting Rik Smith glide around the edge of the forest. "Here comes your young man."

Rik had draped his anti-grav floater with a carpet and had heaped the carpet with cushions amongst which he sat with his feet tucked up on his thighs. He wore a tall black hat, a white undergarment turned down at the neck over a black scarf bunched at the throat and held in place by a pin, a black coat that reached to his knees, pinstripe trousers, black socks and black shoes. A brass buckle hung from his shoulder and a circle of white azaleas lay behind him on the cushions. Mrs. Rubinstein had no idea where he had found the designs for his clothes but she could guess at what they had cost. Ridiculous. "Just look at him!"

Rebecca already was. He looked truly weird. Fantastic. "Hi," she called as he dismounted with a smile lighting his dark face. He carried a gift-wrapped parcel under his arm. A head taller than her father, slim and light-footed, he strolled across the lawn. "Hi there, Mrs. Rubinstein, Professor . . ." He gave Rebecca a peck on the cheek. "Happy birthday, hon. How about trying this on for size." He handed her the parcel. "It's silk."

"But not from China," joked the Professor as his daughter hurried off.

Rik smiled. "What's the book?"

Professor Rubinstein showed him the cover. *RESEARCHES INTO CALITRIATHENETICS OF THE TWELFTH MILLENNIUM ON TERZAR SIX* by Doctor Jean De Vries and Professor Marie Anne Courne.

Rik said, "I've never been sure what Calitriathenetics are."

"Or is," suggested the Professor as he riffled the pages. "Another hundred thousand words and I may be able to tell you."

Their laughter put Mrs. Rubinstein into a worse mood. Men! They were always in alliance.

"That's if you are still interested," the Professor added to Rik as his daughter reappeared in Rik's birthday present. The dress was long, waisted and black. She carried a wisp of black lace in one hand.

"That's a *mantilla*," Rik told her. "You wear it on your head. Well," he added apologetically to her parents, "I guess we should be moving along if we're not going to be late."

"For what?" asked Mrs. Rubinstein.

"The end of the world," Rik said.

Mrs. Rubinstein took his smile as mockery. "How dare you?"

"Well, Ma'm, it's not exactly my doing."

Rebecca stepped in with a conciliatory kiss. "See you later, Mom."

Unmollified by the kiss, her mother said, "See you're back in time for dinner. Uncle Sherry's coming over for present-giving and there's turkey and sweet potatoe pie."

Rik whistled. "With meringue topping! We'll be back, Mrs. Rubinstein."

We'll be back indeed! Glaring at the departing pair, Mrs. Rubinstein fought to control her anger. Inviting himself to dinner like that, the cheek of the *schwartze*. And to celebrate the end of the world. What sort of a remark was that? "I mean, *you* heard him," she said to her husband who had ducked back behind his book. "Benny, I'm *talking* to you. Why didn't you *say* something?"

Her husband checked his timer. "Oh dear, I'm going to be late."

"For the end of the world?"

"World?" Puzzled, the Professor studied his wife. She knew that look. It was the look he wore whenever he found her behavior irrational. Next he would ask whether she was having her period. Let him dare!

But, instead, he said, "No dear, for the faculty meeting at the Dean's office." Mention of the Dean gave him an excuse to look away from his wife and out across the rolling plateau to where the golden domes of the University glowed in the morning sunlight. "I hear young Rik's joining us next semester."

Next semester was still four months away. For

now, Rik slid his floater around the forest and
out across the sweeping ribbon of agricultural
land that supplied food for the small population
of the University planet. Out this direction there
was nothing but the space station. Rebecca arranged a smile on her lips as she squeezed his
hand. Her smile was designed to communicate
a teasing invitation. It was a good smile. She had
practiced it in front of the mirror often over the
last months. "We're going off planet?"

Rik said, "Yes."

"Far?"

There were no atlases of space — or none Rik
had seen outside the museum on Nevin Two.
Distance was an on-planet concept. Once in matter-transfer, a spacer thought in energy tables and
co-ordinates. But Rebecca wasn't a spacer; her
family had lived on University Planet for six generations. "A few galaxies," he said and squeezed
her hand as they dipped over the grassed sound-
bank enclosing the space station.

With University Planet self-supporting and
only exporting research and ideas, the station
bowl was the smallest Rik had seen: a three room
admin building, one workshop, a hangar, a small
workshop and the apron. A pair of hundred ton
shuttles squatted on the apron.

Rik raised a hand in greeting to the old Stationmaster who stood propped against the South
wall of the admin building, a pipe in his mouth.
"Hi there, Mister Calvin. How's the rheuma-
tism?"

"Hi yourself," said the old man. "I checked
your plotting. Not bad for a kid. Your father
would be pleased."

Rik grinned. "He's coming through this way for graduation."

"Yeah? Well, it's always nice to see him," said the Stationmaster. "Anytime you're communicating, you tell him hullo."

"I'll do that, Mister Calvin," said Rik. Slipping an arm round Rebecca's waist and carrying the circle of white azaleas, he followed the old man over to the hangar. There were six personal bugs in the hangar. The Stationmaster's was a blue four-seater with the Inter-Space Transport Agency red eagle and flash painted on each door. "It's real kind of you to loan me transport," Rik said.

"Yes, well see you look after it," the Stationmaster said as Rik and Rebecca buckled in. "Don't hang around on the surface too long and get your ass back here by six. Mrs. Calvin gives me hell if I'm late for supper." Thought of his wife made the old man peer at Rebecca. "This Professor Rubinstein's girl?"

Rik said, "That's right."

"You lose the Professor's girl and I'll lose my pension."

Rik said, "Don't worry," and closed the door before giving Rebecca a wink. "A real old timer," he said.

Old timer or not, being treated as a chattel held no charm for Rebecca. She said, "It was like he thought I couldn't speak."

"That's how they are," Rik said. "Dad's the same." Flipping to anti-grav, he floated the bug clear of the hangar and waved to the old man before lifting into orbit. "How about that?"

The view of University Planet was beautiful, Rebecca admitted, but the Stationmaster's attitude still rankled. Put two men together and it was always the same. What with her pimple, her mother and the old man, her seventeenth birthday was off to a lousy start. Fingering her chin, she said, "We will be back for dinner?"

That was life, Rik thought, as he took in Rebecca's pout. You planned transferring half way across the known Universe and all your girlfriend considered was whether you'd get her home in time for dinner. Maybe his Dad was correct: women were great, but not in space. Certainly Rik's mother had been out of place in space. She had vanished eight months after Rik's birth. She'd left a note. *I'm not cut out for this life.*

With ten thousand and some inhabited planets, searching for her was pointless. The closest they had come was a rumour she had remarried with a shopkeeper on Latmar Twelve.

"So why follow up on it," Rik's father had said. "We find her, we risk messing whatever new life she's managed to build. Weird," he'd added, "your Ma thought marriage to a space prospector would be real romantic. Six months of it and she wanted a country cottage with a lawn and roses spilling over the door."

Weird indeed, Rik thought with another quick glance up from the computer board. Rebecca had gotten her pimple to bleed. "So will we or won't we be back in time?" she prompted.

"Sure we will," Rik said and added, "Picking will make it worse."

Rebecca nearly screamed.

Busy tapping the co-ordinates into the computer, Rik failed to notice how mad he'd got her.

"So here we go," he said, closed the transfer shields and pressed the matter-transfer switch.

The transfer heave caught Rebecca by surprise.

Rik said, "Hang on," as she fought against throwing up. She gained control just in time to be hit by the fallout of transfer. She clamped both hands to her mouth but was too late.

Rik said, "Oh Lord . . ."

Like any Lord could save her dress! It was ruined and she felt ill enough to cry rather than just have tears in her eyes from having been sick.

Rik opened the shields and fumbled a pack of paper towels from beneath the computer board. "Gee, I'm sorry . . ."

Sorry! Mopping at herself, Rebecca peeped down through her tears at the planet they were orbiting. Whatever she had expected, it wasn't a dead chunk of meteorite-pocked rock.

Rik said, "We'll go down for a couple of minutes." He sunk the bug on anti-grav to the surface and extended an atmosphere barrier three meters out before opening the door. "Well, here we are," he said as he swung onto the ground. Pearly gray dust puffed over his shoes and the cuffs of his pants.

Rebecca thought, Big Deal! No airless heap of rocks would shift her out of the bug.

Rik said, "Could you pass the flowers?"

Her dress dragged clamily at her thighs as she reached back for the white azaleas. She would have liked to have thrown them at him but hadn't the strength.

Rik didn't notice her tears. He was busy filling three glass phials with dust. He corked the phials

and returned them to the inside pocket of his coat
before accepting the azaleas.

Laying the wreath against a rock, he unslung
the bugle and, standing heels together and delib-
erately erect, raised the mouthpiece to his lips.

The last long trailing note of the Last Post faded
into the isolation of the dead planet, melancholy
and beautiful. "Well, I guess that's that," he said.

Rebecca had forgotten her pimple and wrecked
dress. He looked so sad and solemn that all she
could think of was taking him in her arms to
comfort him and protect him. She didn't know
what over or what from. She didn't care. She
knew he needed her. That was enough.

"We'd best get going," he said. He lifted the
bug well out beyond the star's grav field before
switching to park. He checked his timer. "We've
a couple of hours to wait."

Rebecca didn't ask what for. She wanted to
draw his head down to her breast but there wasn't
much comfort in throw-up stains. "I'm going to
have to take my dress off," she said. Struggling
out of the silk sheath was difficult in the confined
space of the bug.

Rik said, "I could put the seat backs flat . . ."

Poor dear, Rebecca thought. All his self-assur-
ance had evaporated. She smiled at him, a gentle
smile. Later she would ask what had so upset
him. For now all she said was, "That would be
nice . . ."

Stripped to her breast cups and pants, she said,
"Do we have any water and a cloth?"

Rik damped the handkerchief he wore in his
breast pocket and handed it to Rebecca, his head
turned away in fear of upsetting her by seeming
to watch.

Rebecca smiled her thanks. A stain marred her left cup. Turning her back to Rik, she whispered, "Please . . ." and waited for him to undo the fastenings. His fingers were nervous and incompetent. Rebecca didn't help. She waited . . . then, as the cups came loose, lay back on the flat seats.

"You're so beautiful," Rik whispered.

She opened her arms. "My darling . . ."

Back at the University the Dean's monthly staff meeting had dragged on through luncheon before finally ending. Professor Rubinstein knew they hadn't decided anything. Meetings were not designed for decision making. They were designed to give committee members an added sense of self-importance.

Professor Rubinstein failed to feel important. Threading his way across the quadrangle between groups of young students enjoying the afternoon sun, he felt overweight, useless, aging and out of touch.

Glancing at the golden dome of the library, he met the eyes of a black student watching him from the upper level. Were they really bigger than other men? And what were Rik and Rebecca up to? But he knew what they were up to . . . or what, if they weren't up to yet, they soon would be up to.

It was a classic situation, the Professor admitted: jealousy over one's daughter. *One's daughter!* It was always easier to transfer into the first person impersonal when faced by the personal.

But Rik was a nice kid, studious and intelligent. Some day he would make a fine addition to the University staff . . . and, perhaps, a son-in-law capable of sustaining a decent conversation.

A slight shudder of guilt shook the Professor, guilt over his liking for Rik. Being supportive of Rik was an act of disloyalty to his wife. But so was remaining a Professor when he could command twice the salary by accepting a consultancy with his brother-in-law Sherry's firm of Systems Analysis. No doubt that subject would surface at dinner for the umpteenth time . . .

The end of the world, the Professor thought while looking up at the peaceful hills beyond the University. Being forced to abandon the University for Systems Analysis would certainly be the end of his world. As for Rik . . .

Turning away from his office, the Professor entered the library. "Uhm, ahh . . ." he began.

Every knowledge outlet on the campus was keyed to that opening. "Good afternoon, Professor Rubinstein," responded the library. "What can we do for you?"

The Professor said, "I was wondering . . ."

After the programmed ten seconds, the library said, "Yes, and what were you wondering, Professor?"

Professor Rubinstein was unsure . . . also he wished the library had vocal tone change capability. The library was a non-emotional entity according to its designers. *Can a non-emotional entity indulge in mockery?* he had once asked the library.

Of whom? the library had responded. The Professor had accepted defeat.

Now, he asked, "I was wondering whether anyone has been doing research on mourning dress."

"Richard Alouishas Smith," responded the library after a brief check. "Final year student at

Springland High. Library authority issued by Professor Benjamin Rubinstein. Subject: mourning dress from the planet Terra, late Christian era."

"Thank you," said the Professor.

The library responded, "Our pleasure."

Back in his office, Professor Rubinstein called the Astronomy Department outlet. "The Milky Way galaxy," he began after a couple of ums and ahs. "There's a planet Terra in the Sol One system . . . or, at least, there was, and if the Sol One system still exists, could you give me a situation report?"

So there it was, he thought as the reply came through. For a moment he feared for his daughter's safety . . . but Rik was experienced in space. No, he had no need to worry on that score. Fading the wall to the quadrangle, he watched the students hurrying by. Did they have a sense of direction? Perhaps a belief in direction was man's greatest illusion.

Rising from his chair, the Professor took from a display cabinet the square can which held pride of place in his collection of antiquities. For a while he merely fondled the can lovingly. Then, why not? he decided and called the curator of the University museum with an invitation to afternoon tea. Next he invited the Dean.

Meanwhile, Mrs. Rubinstein had almost finished stuffing the turkey. Thumping in the stuffing, she wished she was thumping Rik Smith. What would her brother Sherry say at finding a schwartze at their dinner table, she with her boastful letters to her brother of how Rebecca was going steady with Abbie Kaufman of the CCT Mining Kaufmans. And now a schwartze!

Oh God, Oh God, she moaned and dug the last of the sage and onion stuffing into the carcass while, fifty galaxies away, her daughter gently guided Rik into touch with her hymen.

"My darling, Oh my darling," whispered Rebecca, "be strong for me . . ."

And the Dean entered the Professor's study. "Heavens," he said on finding the Professor's writing table laid with porcelain cups from the Fourth Ming Dynasty. The Curator had brought them over from the museum.

"We thought this deserved something special," Professor Rubinstein mumbled in embarrassment. He handed the Dean the square can from his collection.

TWININGS QUEEN MARY TEA
a superb hill grown Darjeeling
with Muscatel flavour

"Good God," the Dean said. "It must be over two billion years old."

"And still fresh," murmured the Curator, sipping his appreciation.

"Delicious," agreed the Dean.

Both men looked at Professor Rubinstein.

The Professor blushed. "Well, actually, it is a rather special day . . ." He glanced up at the wall timer. Two minutes to go and Mrs. Rubinstein slid the turkey into the oven. She closed the oven at the exact moment that Sol One went nova. Vast sheets of flame devoured the small dead planet once known as The World, flames that lit the inside of the personal bug and transformed the sweat on Rik's forehead into glowing jewels. As

Rik shuddered to completion, the heavens moved for Rebecca Rubinstein. She knew her parents would never understand . . .

THE REVELATION
by
Thomas M. Disch

Ingman Bergmar was a wretched man. Not for any of the workaday reasons you or I or Job might have offered, such as unrequited love or insufficient funds or boils, but for what seemed to some of his critics a secondary sort of complaint — God's silence. Bergmar wanted God to talk to him the way He'd talked to Moses and Abraham and Adam in the Bible. Not that he believed there'd ever been a historical Moses or Abraham, much less an Adam. He didn't, and that was part of the problem. Actually he would have settled for an angel, even a small Sign, so long as it was genuinely miraculous and not just a bit of luck. He'd always thought the story about Hemingway turning Catholic as a thank-you for being cured of impotence reflected poorly on that anthor's intellectual equipment, nor did he have much respect for Pascal and his wager. If God were up there he should speak out. Nothing less would satisfy Ingman Bergmar.

This challenge to the Almighty had been a recurrent theme in Bergmar's films. From the first frame of the Arctic Tetralogy in the late '40's down to the last anguished whisper of Senta in *The Wolves Are Howling* Bergmar had been making the same non-negotiable demands: speak now or forever hold Your peace. He had repeated Ivan Karamazov's famous poser — how could a just God allow innocent children to suffer? There was no answer. He'd confronted Him with Auschwitz, Hiroshima, the statistics for highway fatalities and terminal cancer. God did not choose to reply. His mistress, two-times Academy-Award-winning Una Thorwald, had committed suicide at the height of her career, and still not one word of consolation or reassurance from on high. Bergmar had come to believe that God didn't exist, that there was nothing but a meaningless mulch of atoms and energy bubbling around in the void utterly indifferent to questions of human fate.

Then God spoke to him.

He spoke to him out of the center of a canolle that Bergmar had brought home from the one good Italian bakery in Stockholm. "Okay, Bergmar," God said (in Swedish), "let's talk."

"Lord!" said Bergmar, putting down his fork on the homey embroidered tablecloth and staring at the canolle in dismay. He knew with *a priori* certainty that it *was* the living God talking to him out of the canolle, but even so he felt compelled to ask: "Is it You?" After a lifetime of taking nothing on faith Bergmar wasn't about to trust to mere intuitions, however powerful.

God assured Bergmar that He was indeed the Everlasting God, Creator of Heaven and Earth, the One and Only King of Kings, and Lord of Lords.

Bergmar didn't know how to continue. Somehow it didn't seem either polite or entirely safe to return to such subjects as suffering children or atomic holocaust. Undoubtedly God, since He evidently did exist, had His own inscrutable reasons for letting such things happen.

"Well?" God insisted.

"I'm not worthy of this," Bergmar ventured, always handy with an appropriate quote.

The canolle seemed to accept this as its due. "So? Neither were the others." Meaning (Bergmar understood) Moses and Abraham and Adam.

"Is there something you'd like me to do, Lord?" Bergmar asked, perhaps a touch too eagerly.

"I think you could eat a more balanced diet," God answered. "Cut out the cholesterol and reduce your starches. Get more roughage. And Vitamin C, at least five hundred milligrams a day. Vitamin C is great stuff."

Bergmar nodded respectfully but also a bit impatiently. Dietary regulation, though a traditional benevolence of the Deity, was not the area he'd hoped for guidance in. "I'll do that. Anything else?"

"I think you might start observing the Sabbath. It's only one day out of the week, after all."

"Absolutely! Anywhere in particular?"

"Wherever you feel comfortable."

"Is that all, Lord? Isn't there some message I could pass on to the world at large?"

"I doubt the world at large would believe you, Ingman. In any case, My prophets have said most of it before. People don't listen. They're iniquitous. You know that."

"Yes, of course, Lord. But I —"

"Iniquitous," the canolle muttered in grieved tones. "And I'll tell you this — I don't intend to put up with it much longer! The fornications and false gods! The additives! The things they show on tv even during the hours when young children might be watching!''

"It is a disgrace, Lord, I know."

"And *you're* one of the worst offenders, Ingman!" He bellowed so that the canolle seemed in danger of exploding all over the breakfast nook.

Then, in a twinkling, He was once again all sweetness and light. "But that's all one. I'll forgive you your trespasses if you'll promise to put an end to them. If you must make movies, make ones the whole family can enjoy watching."

Bergmar promised, though at the same time he wished God would be explicit as to just which aspects of his film-making He objected to. The nudity? Hadn't He created us male and female, and was it sinful to pay a certain respectful attention to the results? Or was it rather the general emotional tone he was objecting to, what one critic had referred to as 'the typical Bergmar blend of stoic distress and quiet, unassuming despair'? That might be harder to remedy, even now. There were still aspects of human existence to complain of, regardless of the long Silence being finally broken. Bergmar wasn't sure he'd ever be able to make a film entirely to his own and the Almighty's liking. The Lord God seemed to have a rather old-fashioned outlook, not to say reactionary. He put Bergmar in mind of his own father, Ole Bergmar, a timber merchant in Sveg. Noting this resemblance didn't lead Bergmar to doubt the objective reality of the manifestation. When God talks to you, you *know* who He is.

God, being all-wise, had followed the drift of Bergmar's thoughts, and His next words were spoken in an admonishing but not unkind tone. "So, what did you think — that I'd sound like Søren Kierkegaard?"

Bergmar shook his head. "No, no. It even makes sense, when you think about it. I just wish —"

"You wish I were more like you. Everyone does, it's human nature. Now you're probably wondering if I'm really like this or just putting on an act to tease you. Haven't you read the Book of Job? Don't you know better than to question My Judgement?"

"Lord, my name is mud: what can I say?" Bergmar replied contritely, though not without a dash of pride at his quick paraphrase of Job's answer to a similar challenge.

God seemed mollified. He continued in a milder vein: "Would you like to know a secret?"

There was nothing in the world Ingman Bergmar wanted more than to know one of God's secrets. He bowed his head reverently, scarcely daring to look at the pastry on the dish before him.

God said: "Lo, in two years this world will come to an end."

"Completely?" Bergmar insisted, astonished. He'd expected a much smaller secret.

"Completely and irrevocably. Kaput — forever!"

"If you don't mind my asking . . . how will it happen?"

"By an entirely natural cataclysm that will satisfy both a moral and a poetic sense of justice."

"A collision with another planet?" Bergmar

guessed, when it appeared the canolle would not elaborate on these very abstract hints.

"No."

"The Bomb?"

"Not that either."

"Some kind of ecological catastrophe, then?"

"No more guessing, Ingman. When the time comes, it will all be clear. Till then, remember: eat right, keep the Sabbath, and love your neighbor while you can."

God said no more.

Bergmar went on looking at the canolle the rest of the afternoon, but the Divine Presence had definitely absconded. The canolle was no more now than an ordinary canolle with a slightly soggy crust. Needless to say, Bergmar found it impossible to consider eating it. He put it into the refrigerator, where gradually, over the course of the next three weeks, it developed a fuzzy green mold. Finally, with a sense of grief and of relief in equal parts, Bergmar put the canolle out with the morning garbage.

Given the more than two year time-lag between the initial inspiration and the final release of any movie, there didn't seem to be much point in starting a new production, even if he'd been able to think of something suitable in the apocalyptic circumstances. Bergmar announced his retirement and returned to his native Sveg. He ate sensibly, attended church every Sunday, learned the names of his neighbors and tried his best to love them.

As the allotted time wore on he did sometimes wonder whether his revelation hadn't been something in the nature of a hallucination. Without

God present and actively inspiring his faith, Bergmar tended to fall back in his old rut of materi-
alistic doubt and ordinary common sense. Could
he ever be certain it had really been God who'd
spoken to him out of the canolle and not just
some quirk of his subconscious? Had the Silence
truly been broken?

When exactly on the day God had predicted,
the world came to an end, Bergmar knew for a
fact that his doubts had been unfounded. It had
been God who'd talked to him. He was annihi-
lated a happy man.

NIRVANA IS A NOWHERE PLACE
by
Joel Schulman

"No way," Fenton screeched over the hotline to the Pearly Gates. "There is absolutely no way we can accommodate three decimal point five billion souls."

"Tough shit, you're going to have to," St. Peter rejoined.

"Negative. We're up to four sets of books as it is, let alone resources. We just had to put white robes on the endangered species list. Haloes have become a luxury item for only the Very Very Holy and The Heavenly Host. We'd like to help, but there's a bottom line."

"Be a nice guy," St. Peter warned. "You know how it is, nobody loves a comptroller anyway."

"I'm doing my job," Fenton said. "I'm just doing my job."

St. Peter laughed until he gasped. "The last thousand guys who got up and told *that* one got sent straight *downstairs*. You preserve your humanity, Fenton, or I'll talk to The Lord about you."

Fenton cringed, but managed to reply. "I *have* my humanity. It's true I once thought of having it out, but I didn't. And I know all about your goody goody schemes."

"Look Dum-Dum," St. Peter fairly growled, "the world is coming to an end! The sky is falling down! Nuclear holocaust! One hundred percent mortality. And you're going to sit there on your bottom line and let it happen."

"You betcher ass," was Fenton's first reaction, because on Earth, as he was in Heaven, Fenton had been generally and quite rationally disliked. It wasn't hard to see why. He had been born tight, rigid, uncool and ungraceful, quick to find fault and slow to let the life around him flow and fly. He had tried to compensate with wise choices of roles. *Profession:* School board comptroller. *Hobby:* Umpiring women's softball games and collecting rare coins. *Last Book Read:* Paradise Lost. *Scotch:* None.

Upon his untimely and relatively unlamented demise at the age of 41, choking on a peach pit after being informed that he was being audited by the IRS, Fenton ascended, somewhat mysteriously, to Heaven. The Lord let him in because he had been, in narrow terms, a good family man, a surprisingly brave and steadfast individual, and as honest as a comptroller can be. More importantly, The Lord sensed some still water running deep and kindly between Fenton's narrow-set black beady eyes, some well-spring of humanity that needed but the celestial tones of the harp and some particular occasion to bring it forth. Also, in his crusty way, Fenton was a good team player.

But when challenged, when cornered by a command to become Mr. Nice Guy, Fenton got up on his pedestal and balked. That's why he said "you betcher ass" to St. Peter. What was the end of the world compared to the preservation of Fenton's reputation as a professional sourpuss? "You betcher ass," he repeated to St. Peter. "I *will* let it happen."

"There is no place for them to go," St. Peter said. "Total thermonuclear disaster. I understand Prometheus is having a barbecue tonight."

"It's not our problem," Fenton said. "We are strictly overpopulated. What's the matter with the other places, anyway?"

"If they belong here, they belong here. As it is written. God said that a long time ago."

"Have you *tried* the other places?" Fenton asked.

"No, and The Lord will not permit it," St. Peter sighed. "Excuse me, someone's just pulled up to the guard shack by the Pearly Gate."

If The Lord says no, then no is the Word. But Fenton felt there was no harm in trying to feel out the others. He put on his striped cap and shoved a stogie between his teeth. It helped put him in the mood for the mock-earthy tone he adopted when talking to heathen. And he pushed the buttons for this unlimited account — 10 cents to call any major city — an authorization number, then dialed area code and number.

"Hello, *Down*Town," he guffawed into the receiver. "Have you heard about the impending thermo-nuke disaster? It's absolute Splitsville for the Earthlings, you know."

"Heard about it?" a deep chuckle responded.

"We paid for it. It's our baby."

"Fine," Fenton said. "Then you take'm. Every last one."

"Baby, you been listening to them harps too long. This is the major leagues. We take the cream of the crop only. Starting one half-hour from now, you gotta be a real badass to get on the roster here."

"One half-hour, hmmm . . . How do I know you're telling the truth?"

"You don't," the chuckle chuckled. "Now ain't that a bitch?"

Fenton hung up on him. He should have known better. He consulted his listings and dialed Nirvana. There was no answer. He hung up and dialed again. This time a recorded message responded. "This is a recorded message. You have reached Nirvana. There is nobody home. Nobody has been home. Nobody will be home. Technically, this is not a working number. You should consult your listings and dial again. However, should you care to leave a message, you may speak cautiously upon the sound of the tone."

Fenton was honestly enraged. "Out to lunch, huh? Spinning your prayer wheels? Too ethereal to speak with a Heavenly Host? Well, hoity-toity. Listen and listen good, punks. Now in half an hour, maybe less, the Earthlings will buy the farm. Every last mother's child of them. Boom Boom. O-U-T. No Satori, just goombye. And we don't have enough room, even for the pure Judeo-Christian types. Now you can play all the games you want, but I know you got nothing there. You got no harps, no houris, no barbecue, no nectar or ambrosia, no nuttin'. Let's face it, Nirvana is a nowhere place. An underdeveloped afterworld. So why don't you take half — say a third . . . a billion, just a billion of the most energetic and skilled emigrants. Then you can start to build you a rep. What say?"

The recorded message said, "This recorded message has reached the fifth dimension. It no longer exists. Be fruitful and multiply yourself, creep."

Fenton wasn't about to give up. Proceeding randomly, he called Valhalla next. "Wodan, Babee . . . hey, uh, how would you like to do something really trippy for a change?"

"No nukes," Wodan said simply.

"So you know about the Earthlings?"

"Of course. Plus we got enough troubles. The Valkyries want equal rights. Someone has stolen our mead recipe. Sorry, Fenton, but. . . ."

"All right," Fenton sighed. "Well, give my best to Thor."

"Convey my regards to Your Boss," Wodan said.

"The Lord? He's OK. Yeah. Will do. Bye."

Fenton's luck scarcely improved when he called station-to-station to Mt. Olympus.

"Fenton?" Cupid giggled into the mouthpiece. "Oh, yes, the straight man from Heaven. How's it hangin,' Harpo? Do you know Earth Angel? Whadd'ya mean, stop kiddin' around?"

"Just what I said," Fenton said. "This is a very serious matter."

"Shaddup. Or I'll tell my mother on you. Now what's so serious awreddy?"

"Just call Whosis. Zeus. Jupiter."

"Sorry, Bub, he's out diddling a swan. You know, I shot an arrow in the air; where it fell I knew not. Where? Now what is it you wanted to know?"

"Do you know — off hand — if you could accommodate about three billion Earthlings?"

"We'd like to help. But Pan is here for the weekend, and you know what that gets into. Look, send them over for the bash if you want, but permanent residence — well, we're awfully low on ambrosia as it is. . . ."

"All right, all right," Fenton said.

Then Fenton dialed the Happy Hunting Ground. "The Great Spirit, please," he said. "Manitou."

"I am sorry, but the number to which you are speaking has been disconnected."

"Is there a number it has been changed to?"

"No, Sir. But it says 'Gone fishing. Temporary absence. Will return post-holocaust.' "

"Ah, er, thank you, Operator."

"It's nothing, Mr. Fenton. You should come over and see my wing collection some time though, a nice big strong fella like yourself."

"Thank you, Operator. Now will you get me Lao Tzu?"

"Yes, Sir. Stand by."

"Heaven is a state of mind," Lao Tzu said clear as his reflection in the pond. "You cannot consider heaven in material terms."

"There's three and a half bil coming any minute now. How many can you handle at your place?"

"You cannot think in terms of handling or places."

"That's the Way," Fenton said. "Thanks anyway."

Fenton went on. He didn't give up easily. He spoke with Krishna. He spoke with Kali. He spoke with Huitzilopochtli, the hero, and Tonacacihuatl, The Lady of Our Subsistence; with Isis and Osiris, Tara, and Demeter and Kore; Artemis, Pluto, Neptune, and Theseus; Tlazolteotl the Earth Goddess, and some wrong numbers.

Nobody had room for so many as ten souls, let alone the three billion that would be coming.

There was nothing to do but go to God about it. Let's face it; it was his decision anyway. But on the way, in the Celestial Passageway, he happened upon Jesus. "Jesus Christ Almighty," Fenton exclaimed, "do you think we can accommodate the three billion Earthlings?"

Jesus smiled. "In my Father's house there are many rooms."

Fenton smiled. "Of course, Jesus; of course." And it came to pass that Fenton also came upon Muhammed, who was driving a camel down the corridor, carefully staying within the right lane. "Muhammed," he asked. "Do you think The Lord will tell us to take care of the three billion Earthlings?"

"There is no god save Allah, and Muhammed is His Prophet. Allah will do what is necessary."

"Thank you, Muhammed," Fenton said.

Then he went in to the throne room. Abraham was prostrated on the floor, asking God to spare Earth if he could only find ten good men on the planet.

"Get up, Abraham," The Lord spake, "and don't be ridiculous. This isn't the old days. This is all-out thermonuclear war. It's out of my hands."

"But . . ."

"Shut up, Dummy," The Lord said. "Now, I would spare them — if I could. But I can't. They will blow themselves up because they have the weapons to do it. I can control only their hereafter."

"What will you do about it, My Lord?" Fenton inquired.

"Well, Fella, technically it's your decision," replied The Lord, with the bluff broad grin he had learned only recently since Nelson Rockefeller had moved in and bought the heaven next door.

And this is precisely when the urge to be a good guy seized Fenton with all the zeal of the convert, when he gave up his nit-picker of a ghost and let his spirit rise to the actual heaven from whence he'd come for lo these many years. "We can't leave them in Limbo, Lord, 'twouldn't be fair! And the Other Places just can't handle them, though we all of us will do our best. Lord, let them all in! Even the sinners; *I'll* stand up for the sinners. I'll welcome them with every ounce of spirit I can summon. And they shall be fed well, too, and washed in the blood of the Lamb. And they shall on honeydew feed, and drink the milk of Paradise."

And The Lord said, "Hey, Fella . . . Fens, that's what I've wanted to understand about you for a long time. Whether you had it in you. Fens . . . you're full of compassion for your fellows. You are now an official Heavenly Good Guy."

A teardrop fell from each of Fenton's glistening eyes, and the third eye in his forehead, the plenopituitary, as it were, vibrated with Hosannahs, Satori, Epiphany, Recognition, and Expanded Consciousness.

And The Lord smiled, for of course his judgment of Fenton had been vindicated. And the Heavenly Host beamed with acceptance.

And just when Fenton was about to peak in his bliss, just when he was about to ask The Lord how he should minister to three point five billion souls, well just at that absolute instant, to be perfectly frank about it . . . the world came to an end. Which of course was not a complete shock to The Lord and His Circle.

And The Lord beamed with illumination, for He thought of Fenton. Fenton who would never never know how impossible it was for a confirmed Scrooge to shed his skin and conduct himself with generosity. The road to Heaven, no less than Hell, has been paved with sweet but ineffectual resolutions. Such was Fenton's.

But he would never never know, because a second after the world came to an end, Heaven fell as well. Some imaginary demarcational line between material and spiritual phenomena had been breached by the endlessly chained reactions of the split atoms. God, His Godhead conscious at the peak of His Form, knew the end was coming, and it came for Heaven, as it did for Paradise, Hell, Valhalla, and all other Thereafters.

Everything came to an end. Nirvana became a truly nowhere place.

Everything came to an end. Including Fenton, who went out a winner, never imagining how many Earthlings he would have tried to help but sooner or later bureaucratized. And who knows, maybe, had it all gone on, maybe he would have remained high in the congregation of the righteous.

HEIR
by
J. A. Lawrence

This story is dedicated to Ursula Le Guin

I.

Is make symbolical idiomatical effort
Is record many times patience and glory
Learning to new sharing
Difficult

$$427^{2.8795673}$$

II.

Progress in symbolical mandibulation
We Thumid $427^{2.8795673}$ construct statements.
We name symbols. WORDS. Patterns. New-hatched, no control.
Beautiful. Difficult.

Thumid $427^{2.8795673}$ Thumid

III.

We are 2,987,563 bodies. Mighty Rhrh-House of Thumid! Rhrh, the Great and Fertile Mother and queen of the House of Thumid!

We Thumid $427^{2.8795673}$ consort of Rhrh-House of Thumid walk in the Out. No. Untruth. Sentries

walk in the Out. Thumid. Symbols confuse. We.
I? This body. These bodies. One? 2,987,563?

Out. Brightlight is hidden. Warmness and wetness. Beautiful.

Thumid 427$^{2.8795673}$

IV.

Do you receive these symbols, Rhrh? She stirs
and comforts. Rhrh? No body of this House has
leisures. We-I trouble ourself with new learnings.
Rhrh is occupied with eggs. Brightlight still hides
and warmness comes.

This bodies revel in Out-longings.

Thumid 427$^{2.8795673}$

V.

Uneasiness within this father-body. Many young
grow armors. War will come. Her Great Fertility
Rhrh knows all matters before their time. But. If
we grow armors, so also the enemy. Uneasiness.

Thumid 427$^{2.8795673}$

VI.

At last I understand! I. I. I am Thumid
427$^{2.8795673}$, WE are the Rhrh-House. I. I. I. I, father
to the Rhrh-House. 3,081,429 bodies are children
to Rhrh and Thumid of the Rhrh-House. Oh, great
is the Rhrh-House of Thumid!

Beautiful.

I, THUMID 427$^{2.8795673}$

VII.

Great Rhrh slumbers among the small white
children and her attendants. These things, symbols, please her, as a gift of feather-strokes. Never-

theless, we know our thoughts together in the usual way. She exudes sweetness.

Only I, Thumid 427$^{2.8795673}$ know of symbols. This is unright. Sharing must. Children must.

Builders increase. Rhrh-House grows warm, very warm, and busy to make larger the channels for wind. One time ago so many channels made coldness in the House; now each darktime finds more needed.

It has come to me to stir a Remembrance. The young have not remembered since the last Wing Days. Perhaps these new symbols will clear the remembering, and the inheritance of patience and glory be even more alive.

Oh, Rhrh-House of Thumid, hear and honor!

I am making symbols as well as knowing. The House murmurs, those within and those abroad.

Oh, House of Thumid, hear and honor!

The Great and Fertile mother drowses, but drops of Bright Remembrance ooze from her noble belly.

Remember, remember. . . .

. . . The rocks were rich with plants, the pale plants that grow within bite-reach. No Brightlight blinded, and the air was filled with tangy perfumes. All was the domain of Ap, Ap the Glorious, Ap the Forever, in the First House of the First Home, and behold, it was very good. No giant vermin infested that garden, pursuing and trampling. Our strong bodies were clothed in breathing shells and we danced in twilight days. Food, comfort, warmth and love blessed the House of Ap. Places of small warm waters comforted the long long days of many generations.

. . . Remember the fire-time and the burning rock. Remember the bursting of gardens into mountains of flame. Remember the smoke and the clouds and the dry water places. Remember, oh, remember, Ap the Deathless and the mind we share.

. . . Remember. Dust blew and covered the light and our eyes burned.

Rhrh stirs, her time is on her. We must leave the Remembrance for now. New eggs need attention and the nurses prepare to kiss the returning House with ready food. I am hungry.

VIII.

A gardener scurries in and touches my antennae. The enemy is approaching the House. The first are already in the gardens.

Shepherds rush past, herding the animals to their pens. Trenga beetles are always slow. Soldiers pour out of the corridors, their slicers stiffly held, ready to cut down the odious wreckers that assault our peace.

I hear the sound of battle far away under the house. There are few thoughts to spare for reporting, but it seems that the enemy are strangely weak. They stagger without wounds. All order has departed from them — they are attacking as savagely as ever, and falling untouched. The Lodgers' cadre is knocking them off their feet with ease.

It is a rout!

The jubilant army returns, carrying captives and loot; seeds, new animals for the pens, cleanerbugs. The servants run to them with strokings and food, and offer the eating-kiss joyfully. Rhrh is successfully delivered of the eggs, and all is well in the House.

I, Thumid, will now inspect the gardens.

IX.

I. I. These symbols will not let me rest. A symbol for the Myrmig, the enemy so like and so unlike ourselves. Lazy. Their guards sleep on duty. They are mad for sweets and will do anything for honey. Yet they keep gardens, build — badly — Houses, honor their queen. Fierce fighters, but stupid; they will walk in circles until dead if their leaders are misled. They talk too much.

I do not think they have a First Home to remember. They have hard skins and do not mind Brightlight.

Again today there is no Brightlight. Darktime changes to dim and back, and it is not painful to be abroad.

I would like to think a thought only in symbols, and keep it within this body. A private thought. I WISH I HAD REALLY SEEN FIRST HOME.

There is no murmuring. Perhaps no other body knew that thought? Not even dearest Rhrh.

It is true, then. Thoughts symbolized are thoughts alone.

ALONE. I. These are strange comfortless symbols. I must go to Rhrh, quickly. Thumid $427^{2.8795673}$ of the Rhrh-House of Thumid. Not ALONE.

, , , , , , , , , , , , , , ,

X.

Symbols are not all pleasant. Fear. Sadness. No other body but this one knows sadness.

Almost all of the new children have eyes. I was the only one of my generation. We have not needed them in the warm dark Houses. Is the Brightlight dead, then?

A sadness. Some of the young develop wing-pads. They will leave us, the princes and princesses of the House of Thumid. This has always happened in its season. Why do I feel sadness?

It is warm in the Out, and moist. If only the Brightlight would never come back!

XI.

There are times that call our greatness into a new phase. I sense that one of these is coming. There are changes everywhere.

Nine and seventy times the leaves have gone dead and cold and been reborn since Thumid $427^{2.8795673}$ and the Great and Fertile Rhrh came to this place and founded the Rhrh-House. Nevertheless, it seems such a short time since our Days of Wings and our mating flight . . .

. . . Rhrh, my sister, slender of waist and so swift in the air — have you forgotten? Eight and seventy leaf-comings you have seemed content, lying in your chamber with your companions and our children — how many, my love? Five hundred million? More?

Can one create symbols for parts of oneself? Rhrh is a symbol, a sound, a humming, a warmth.

Once I went and walked in the Out; I can walk, though dear Rhrh does not stir from her chamber.

I became hungry. Among the tidbits that lie under
the freshplants — leaves, old woods, aromatic
lost buds — there was an odd pale leafthing. I
took a mouthful of the crackling substance. A
new and thrilling taste! Like wood, but with a
flavor of — of — I have no name for these things.
I was replete.

I noticed something. Where I had browsed with
such delight there were unveinlike markings,
black shapes. I climbed on to what was left of the
leaflike thing and inspected them closely. With
a suddenness I awoke. They were symbols. They
meant something that they were not, something
new and alien, incomprehensible and fascinat-
ing. I stared around me, wondering which tree
had taken to symbolizing upon its leaves. They
looked as they always did, immensely tall, dripping with the wetness that sometimes falls from
up. None had pale leaves.

I wanted to understand. No hunger has ever
seized me so completely. The strange leaf was
disintegrating in the wetness. I knew then that
this thing must be done. These black symbols
were dying — but I would make my own!

That day, a small part of me was separated from
the House. Frightened, I scuttled back to Rhrh as
fast as my legs would go and hurled myself into
her chamber. She woke, and greeted me, expecting the usual mating; but I could only snuggle
close to her warm bulk. Gradually calm returned
and I was able to function.

The Queen exudes the stimulus for whatever
the House will need.

My sleep was tormented by symbols, blackly
drifting in a void of loneliness. I awoke, dry all

over, many times. I named Fear; the House of isolation where my appetites were leading me.

But one can get used to anything, as has been proved.

XII.

It grows harder to synchronize with the House. My old body is too small for all this novelty.

ALONE. FEAR. I.

Rhrh oozes Bright Remembrance. I will sink my Fear in remembering the patience and the glory of the House of Ap. The Great Transudation must be refreshed in the House.

Oh, House of Thumid, remember!

In First Home, our bodies were different. We too had skins of bone. Our selves lived in the place of warmcloud, until the burning time.

The burning time came slowly. There was no water, except for a few tunnels that exuded moisture. Then it was that Ap the Builder, who was our self, taught us of Houses. There we created the House of utter design, whose walls were thick to protect us from the heat, and whose air traps were cunning to cool the air that circulated in the House. Plants grew within the walls, the pale plants that grow within bite-reach, and nourished us.

But the burning times came again, and each return was harder. The waters boiled away. The air scorched our bellies. The Apqueen exuded, and we began to change. Our air-tubes enlarged with each generation until they could suck the small goodness from the air, and their linings grew hard against the heat. Ap saw the thickening of the clouds, and they too were boiling.

We left the Great House, and fled, learning to sail the winds, seeking water in the clouds higher toward the up.

The waters retreated further into the up, and we followed. Bodies of the House grew strong hard wings to ride the winds, and armorskin against the flamedrops in the lower levels.

The waters of the clouds became strong. Little food grew anywhere among the burning rocks. All things tasted of the yellow rock that sickens.

Then it was that Ap the Changer and his Queen, the Immortal Apqueen, formed us yet again. The choking air entered our breathing tubes and we grew sacs to filter and store the air within us. We learned to hurl our selves higher and higher among the clouds, spewing the exhausted air behind us. Our amorskins began to feel chilled and tight and breathing froze our air tubes. The Apqueen labored, and we grew underskins of spongy cells that warmed our bodies. We became small and compact inside our complex double shells.

Higher and higher we sailed, carrying our gardens with us. Many bodies burst through these long ordeals, when we were being expelled from First Home. The air was thin for breathing and thick for living, saturated with bitter waters. The land far below was scorched and dry, invisible in the steaming cloud.

First Home was dying. We could adapt no more.

Then it was that Ap became the Deathless.

Remember, oh, remember, Oh House of Thumid, the generations of preparing for the Great Transudation!

Rhrh's eggs are few this time. It became necessary to punish one of my sons, whose evening honoring was weak.

XIII.

It is strange. The Bright Remembrance we share with Rhrh is vivid, detailed. Yet the passing of the pale leaflike thing that I tasted so long ago is mine alone, and dim. These one-memories are as sand without clay, they trickle away. I am thinking again of this matter of symbols. I cannot share them with any body. Rhrh is amused, but does not really care. Even the princes turn to other toys.

Remember, oh, House of Thumid!

Remember how it came to Ap that the House of Ap must escape from the First Home. Remember the expulsion from our garden, to the smoke and clouds, to the pain and the burning.

A few spores of food, hoarded and preserved from the days of Building; one young queen, in the first day of her mating; a seed, a spore, a shell composed of the clay from our bodies, with walls as thin as wings. A thousand billion bodies bore these frail cradles up and up, into the thin cold wind layers. One last mighty discharge of all the overdeveloped air sacs we had grown in the past generations of airborne life, and a thousand billion bodies fell exhausted, exploded, back through the clouds. Tiny seedcases of Ap hurled free above the clouds.

Millions rained down again through the winds and burning waters. Tens only never returned to perish in the First Home.

When it was clear that seedships containing

Apqueens had escaped the pull of First Home,
the eggs came. More died; their empty ships
moved on. Their last thoughts cried out; whatever lay beyond the walls was wholly evil.

The living queens had many tasks. The eggs,
the all-important eggs, must be cared for. She
must prepare the building of the House, and tend
the spores. She planted these on the first heap
of eaten clay; the only time that it was not possible to process the clay four times. The second
heap was quickly spread over the thin walls to
make them thick and strong. The spores grew
quickly, with the exudations of the queen, and
made air balance between the walls.

The eggs were slow in coming, and few. In the
coldness she labored, The Apqueen, our great
Mother, huddling close to the spores as they
sprouted. Spores took root in the walls. The
queen died in a nest of food-plants, in the
warmth and friendliness of their fronds. The eggs
hatched, already remembering how to tend the
garden — and the Holy Thrift. There must be no
wasting at all. They ate the body of the queen
and grew strong; they ate all foods four times, to
extract all nourishment, and only the final clay
was used to build the ship. This we have done
ever since; it is our preservation.

They built. There must be a true House. A tiny
hole was bored in the shell. Instantly, ready clay
was slapped over the hole. More and more of the
precious material was pressed through the hole.
Later, when this had dried, the builders exca-
vated a new chamber. The dust they had removed was used to feed the garden on the walls.

A few bodies of Ap thrived. It was no longer possible to know the thoughts of others in each seedship; they had drifted too far apart. Each ship became its own House, and multiplied. Here was born the House of Thumid. We changed again, and became soft, and loved the darkness. We tended the gardens, and built. The ship had four thousand eight hundred and thirty-seven chambers when it burned.

On what wind it rode here from First Home there is no knowing. Remember, Oh House of Thumid, the sudden moving after generations of stillness. Remember the hot walls of the outer chambers, and the burning redness. Remember the Queen of the House, consuming her body in exuding the old patterns of breathing in the heat, trying to hurriedly impose this upon our softened bodies. The burning and the fall occurred abruptly; there was no preparation.

The four thousand chambers broke apart and the careful walls burned. Bodies fell from the chambers into strange searing cloud. Bodies fell, drifting through hot, through wet, into warm and moist, chill and dry. Feeble wings spread; wings burned away.

Remember the spores that a scattered few nurses clung to in their fall. Remember the wetness of earth against poor unshielded bodies, for the armor of First Home was gone for ever. Remember the rich tastes of strange leaves, of lichens; and remember the interminable famine in the midst of plenty.

Of the mouthful who landed, only a fraction survived; those who had come to rest near one

*who held spores. Oh, remember the millions who
died, and the perishing of Ap the Deathless, who
was ourself.*

The spores grew. Slowly. A long hungry time
passed before there were enough bodies to be a
true House. We lived hidden in the ground, and
waited. Our wings were gone; only the Wing Days
of mating were left to us. We were Thumid, the
new House of Thumid, the First House of Thumid,
poor and waiting.

Young came. Queens lived a few comings-of-
leaves only, exhausting themselves with eggs.
The spores grew very slowly.

Oh, remember, remember Thumid the 71st of
the House of Thumid, the small white prince who
drank from the hidden pool. Remember the small
Thumid who ate of the foodless tree-legs, and
did not starve.

Oh, those hidden waters, steamy and splendid!
Waters filled with tiny animals, whose presence
we tried to ignore in our thirsts — and one of
whom was eaten by Thumid 71. We drank those
waters, and we could eat of the fallen tree-legs,
and we lived. We grew larger, and mighty became
the House of Thumid!

Remember the scorching horror of Brightlight
which made us Blind, and from which we hide
ourselves. Remember our tender skins, and the
foul air, and the great Building. Remember the
patterns of the Houses, as we multiplied and
built in new places. Remember the strong walls,
the thick walls, to trap sufficient out-breathings
to make the air good within. Remember the mating flights, and the new Houses among the ferns

and steamy waters. Remember the wandering, and the fleeing.

Remember the monsters of hard skins and of soft, who trampled the plants and crushed them for us, and who crushed us under their feet; the mountains who walked and roared and destroyed our Houses in their passing. Remember the Congenerates, the Other House of Ap, who kept their bone-skins (o fortunate ones), who found the small animals in the waters in another place, and who also hate Brightlight. Pity the Congenerates, who have no Houses and no Bright Remembrance.

Remember the stirrings of the ground, and the times of burning that came also here; remember long suffocation in the thickening air, as more and more trees sprouted behind the burnings. Remember the bitter waters that covered the land, and the crawling giants that came out of the waters. Remember the long sticky-tongues that swept queens, soldiers, builders and children screaming into the maw of a mountain.

Remember the dangers and the enemies we have survived, Oh, House of Thumid. Remember the long long story of Ap the Deathless and our House.

Perhaps I have been pursuing falseness. I thought that this thing of symbols that came to me might be a sign for the future of the House, that Thumid might need the skill. But it did not come from Rhrh, and must be unnecessary. I do not know why it came upon me, for it has brought sorrow with its pleasures.

The Great Transudation took place 37,539,984

generations ago, and is still living in us.
... 422,380,962 comings-of-leaves ... The others know this, but do not care. I alone feel the
passing of time as a reality.

Rhrh knows the needs of the future, but not the
future. What *will come* is unreal to my kind, and
a nonthought. What *has come* is a Bright Remembrance. I think I am an error, and when I am
gone, no symbols will exist again.

Sadness.

XIV.

Now I know the source of sadness. Changes are
coming indeed.

Rhrh is dead.

Soon, beloved Rhrh, I follow. I, I, Thumid
$427^{2.8795673}$ will soon not be. What will become of
this me that I have symbolized? I. ALONE. DIE.

No body of any House fears death. The House
is eternal.

ALONE. I. DIE.

These thoughts that are couched in symbols
are not shared; nonthoughts. Thumid $53^{1.3896805}$
and Ryx the new Queen of the House stare at me
with new-shaped eyes that tolerate the faded
light of Out, and think House thoughts.

We have not seen the Brightlight for seven comings-of-leaves. The air is as comfortable as the
inside of the House, tangy and fresh with out-
breathing. It is beautifully dark. I regret that I,
Thumid, will not have the time to discover the
reasons for all things.

The Myrmig are gone too. Others that trampled
and made loud sounds are also gone, even the
sticky-tongues. And the filthy animals that made
houses of food, and buried their good clay. I think

the young are right. They will not need symbols in this changed place, which is like the Bright Remembrance of First Home; pale plants that grow low in bite-reach are everywhere and there are places of warm small waters. It has come: my secret wish to see First Home has been granted, nearly enough.

There will be no remembering with the children about the comings-of-leaves that did not come because of the white coldnesses, from which we had to flee and separate; no time for re-knowing all the patterns of building that developed with the changing hots and colds and winds; nor the treasurings of water in dry times, nor the repelling of water in wet times; nor how we came to keep the animals, nor the coming of the Lodgers, nor the history of slavery among the Myrmig, nor the love of unbuilding of wood to make good clay. These things will be Brightly Remembered in the Ryx-House of Thumid, among the children.

I wonder still who made the white symbol-leaf. Whoever they were, no doubt they have gone with the rest.

It is time to make my last return to the House, where they will kill me. It is time.

The House of Thumid is deathless.

I. DIE. ALONE.

AFTERWORD

Several elements of the above story which seem to be fiction are not; I would like to list a few facts for the readers.

Characteristics of various species of termites include the following: Fossils of both these and their cousins the cockroaches have been found in Carboniferous deposits, originating about 340,000,000 years ago. Among both of these, certain species live on wood — and cannot digest it without the aid of a symbiotic protozoan. Termites build elaborate nests, designed for the weather where they are located, and which have systems of climate-control through shape, roofings, and air-ducts which are in a constant state of alteration. Other insects often share the nests, and are called termitophiles. The building material is often earth or sand, cemented with excreta — that which remains when the termites have eaten every meal several times over. The nest atmosphere is kept at 5–15% CO_2 — normal air contains about .03%. They are often blind, and always uncomfortable, if not fatally ill, in sunlight. They practice lifetime monogamy between king and queen, and she emits a "social hormone" that regulates the development of the larvae into soldiers, workers or reproductives.

In other words, they operate a near-spaceship economy, and do not seem to be fit for life on earth.

THE KINGDOM OF O'RYAN
by
Bob Shaw

The well-dressed stranger sat down, put his attaché case on the floor, crossed his legs and said, "Is there any insanity in your family?"

I thought immediately of my cousin Trev, who at that very moment was in the next office, squatting inside a packing case lined with aluminum foil and projecting reverent thoughts in the general direction of the star Betelgeuse. Had he finally stepped over the borderline between tolerable nuttiness and criminal lunacy? Was somebody coming to take him away?

"Insanity?" I gave the stranger an indignant stare. "What a ridiculous question! Has anybody filed a complaint?"

"Don't get me wrong, Mr. Cluny." He smiled and took a business card from his vest pocket. "I was merely trying to find out if your views on insanity coincide with mine. You see, I divide the insane into only two categories — the unpredictable and the predictable."

"Do you?"

"Or, to put it another way — the unprofitable and the potentially profitable."

"Really?" I glanced at the card he had handed me. It read: *Ralph D. Wynter, Computer Systems Consultant.* The after-effects of the previous night's binge were impairing my ability to think, but I was practically certain that Wynter wasn't making any kind of sense. "I'm afraid I don't quite see . . ."

"In here," Wynter said impressively, patting his attaché case, "I have a list of the names and addresses of 400,000 crazy people, and it's worth a lot of money to you and me."

"That's good to know." I tried to sound mildly interested and cheerful as I withdrew my legs from the kneehole of my desk just in case it became necessary to flee. Wynter was about forty, with steel-rimmed glasses and a look of square-jawed integrity which would have made him a champion used car salesman, but it was becoming obvious that he had a screw loose. What a way to start the day! I was closeted in my office with a genuine noodle, and the only person I could have called upon for help was my cousin Trev, selfstyled apostle of the Supreme Nizam of Betelgeuse.

Wynter's eyes twinkled behind curved flakes of glass. "You must be wondering what this is all about. Let me make it clear to you by asking one question — do you ever bet the horses?"

"What?" I gazed at Wynter with increased perplexity. This was what he called making it clear?

"Do you ever gamble on horse-racing?"

"Never."

"Why not?"

"Ah . . ." I strove for a succinct way to express my feelings about the evils of gambling. "I might lose my money."

"Good man!" Wynter gave me a delighted grin. "I thought you would have the right attitude, but I wanted to be sure. You see, the crazy people on my list all suffer from the same delusion — they're convinced it is possible to predict the outcome of a horse race."

"That *is* crazy," I replied, beginning to relax a little as I sensed that Wynter was not completely adrift from reality and that he was in fact working round, albeit in a peculiar manner, to making some kind of a proposition. "If there was any way of knowing the winners in advance the profession of bookmaker would never have arisen."

"Precisely! I can see we're going to hit it off just fine."

"I don't think so, Mr. Wynter," I said, flipping his business card back across my desk. "I don't know what all this has to do with computer systems, but I'm a very busy man and I haven't got time to . . ."

"To make yourself a third of a million dollars in less than a month? Tax free?"

My heart wobbled a couple of times like a machine with a defective mounting, and to gain a bit of leeway I said, "I always pay my taxes."

That was a lie, of course. The main reason I allowed cousin Trev to stay on in the business was that he was down in the books as receiving a vice-presidential salary of 25,000 dollars a year, whereas he was able to get by quite comfortably on the sixty a week I actually doled out to him. It was tricks like that which enabled me to keep the place on its feet, but even so things were beginning to look pretty bleak and the notion of making a quick killing had a powerful appeal.

Wynter gave me a knowing glance. "What I

mean is that the money will be untraceable, and it will be up to you whether you declare it or not."

"What money? What is this?"

"Before we go into that, you've got to understand fully the nature of the insanity which afflicts compulsive gamblers." Wynter straightened out his legs and hooked his thumbs into his vest pockets, becoming expansive as he reached a well-rehearsed part of his spiel. "They actually suffer from *two* delusions, two fantasies which complement and reinforce each other. The first one we've already covered; the second follows on logically from the first — namely that within the horse-racing fraternity there is a select group whose members are kept informed of *all* the hidden variables which affect horses' performances, and who therefore know the result of every race in advance.

"The members of this group are supposed to be a kind of Ouspenskian elite, and the idea that they exist comforts the gambler and prevents him from crashing into the stone wall of reality when the horse he expected to win comes in fourth and costs him a lot of money. His calculations were based on the form book and were correct as far as they went, you see, but the Big Boys knew better because they had access to inside information. It's like a religion — but in place of a Messiah the gambler dreams of a benign Big Boy who will take a special liking to him and pass on crumbs of his esoteric knowledge.

"There's no denying the power of the dream. I've seen a crowded bar emptied in thirty seconds because somebody came in and gave a tip straight from the quote horse's mouth unquote. It doesn't matter how shabby and unlikely the tipster may be, it doesn't even matter for the moment that the whole principle of exclusiveness is being violated — every punter there gets the feeling that he has at last been let in on something and he scuttles off to bet his rent money. Even when the horse loses, as it always does, his faith in the omniscience of the Big Boys isn't shaken — he realises he has allowed himself to be deceived by a false prophet and is being punished accordingly."

"It really is pathetic," I said, "but I still don't . . ." I broke off as Wynter leaned forward, eyes flaring whitely, and aimed his index finger at the bridge of my nose.

"You and I are going to make that dream come true for a large group of compulsive gamblers." Wynter's voice was vibrant with evangelistic fervour. "And we're going to charge them an appropriate fee for our services."

I sneered. "A third of a million!"

"For each of us, after we clear our expenses."

The mention of expenses set off subliminal alarms in my mind, but by then I was pretty well hooked, the more so because I had guessed the general nature of Wynter's plan. I'd say that most people have at some stage in their mental development been intrigued by the story about the man who invents chess for the amusement of an ancient king. He refuses the bags of gold offered as payment, and instead asks for one grain of wheat for the first square on the board, two for the second, four for the third and so on, doubling up every time, and the punchline is that by the time they reach the sixty-fourth square all the granaries in the land are unable to cope with the amount of wheat involved. It's a short step from there to putting that kind of mathematics into reverse and playing around with a dwindling series of numbers, and almost the first notion people come to is that of the seemingly infallible prediction.

I nodded at Wynter's attaché case and said, "How many names are on your list?"

"Very good, Mr. Cluny," he replied. "I knew we'd hit it off together. I've got a total of 400,000 names and addresses."

"How do you know they're the right sort of prospects?"

"The United States, Canadian and Quebec governments have been collaborating on a coast-to-coast study of the social consequences of chronic gambling. I was involved with the data storage and retrieval system, and I managed to get a printout of the master list. It cost me a lot of money to grease the right palms, but I got what I needed." Wynter picked up his case and opened it, revealing a massive block of closely printed sheets.

I nodded. "What sort of break down were you thinking of?"

"Well, I plan to use only four-horse and five-horse races." He was speaking quickly now, giving the impression of a man who was as much obsessed as any of his prospective victims. "There was a temptation to include a couple of three-horse races to boost the size of the final tiers, but with three horses it would look too easy. There wouldn't be the same build-up of credibility."

"I'm with you. Go on."

"We start with a four-horse race and send letters to everybody on the list, introducing them to an exclusive new tipster service which is so confident of its results that it won't introduce any charges for the service until it has given four consecutive winners. That should convince them of our honesty and integrity. Naturally, we divide the list into four blocks of 100,000 and tip a different horse to each. When the race is over, regardless of the result, we'll have 100,000 punters on whom we have created an initial good impression, and we forget about the others.

"We take a five-horse race next and do the same kind of thing, leaving us with 20,000 hopefuls to whom we've given two winners. Another four-horse job boils it down to 5,000, and another one gives us 1,250 clients who have had four straight winners and by this time are convinced they've got a hot line to the Secret Masters of the Turf — and that's when we start introducing a modest fee. I'd say two hundred bucks each for the next tip, giving us a first rake-off of 250,000 dollars."

"Two hundred each," I said, slightly taken aback. "That's stinging them a bit, isn't it?"

"Nonsense! The way these people bet they'll have picked up a bundle on their four winners. That's the beauty of the scheme — nobody really gets hurt." Wynter paused to dab flecks of froth from the corners of his mouth. "A five-horse race will reduce them to 250 clients who have had five straight winners, and that's where we advise them that we're being pressured by various powerful organisations who resent our helping ordinary gamblers and want us to suspend our operation."

"Huh?"

"That is vital to the whole plan. It's psychol-

ogy, you see. We build up their hopes and
dreams, then make as though we're going to dash
the cup from their lips. They'll see the pearly
gates swinging shut in their faces and they'll do
anything to squeeze through the gap. So we tell
them that, in view of the great personal risk to
ourselves, it's no longer worth carrying on with
the service unless we can interest really dedicated gamblers who are prepared to pay 2,000
dollars a time for guaranteed winners."

"Two grand!" I began to get a cold feeling in
my stomach.

"Think big, man. The people on my list are
reasonably well heeled and they have compul-
sions. The higher the threshold figure we name
the more determined they'll be to get in on it.
That's the way they think. For a brief golden hour
in their lives they'll have known what it is like
to be on the same side as the all-powerful Big
Boys, and that's a feeling they won't want to re-
linquish. I guarantee they'll come through with
the money — and that will give us a second rake-
off of 500,000 dollars. If it's a five-horse race
they'll be reduced to fifty people who have had
six straight winners and who will be putty in our
hands. I wouldn't want to take undue advantage,
of course, so if we stick to the agreed two grand
per tip we'll pick off a third haul of 100,000. By
then we'll be down to about ten people and well
into a diminishing returns situation, but it means
that sending out a mere ten letters will net us a
useful 20,000 dollars. Add that lot up."

"I already did — it comes to 870,000." I swal-
lowed to ease the dryness in my mouth. "But
these figures are too good, aren't they? It can't
work out as perfect as that."

"Oh, there's bound to be a certain amount of wastage and falling by the wayside," Wynter said unconcernedly, "but I've only been outlining the basics of the idea. In the actual event I would expect to revive clients who had four winners followed by one loser. Tell them it was the fault of the opposition and offer to let them have future tips at half price. That should bring in more than enough to compensate for erosion in the various tiers and leave some over to offset against expenses."

Expenses. There was that word again. I mulled it over for a moment and said, "I get the feeling you didn't pick me purely at random."

"Of course not! I had to find somebody who controlled a mailing services outfit. It had to be big enough to cope with the first mailing shot, but small enough to keep a lot of nosy employees from screwing things up. It also had to be a place that wasn't doing too well — so that the owner would be properly receptive to a good idea."

"Hold it right there," I snapped, squaring my shoulders. "What gave you the idea that . . .?"

He silenced me by holding up one hand, palm outwards, and putting on a world-weary smile. "Don't waste our time with all that stuff, Desmond. I've done my homework very thoroughly and I know *exactly* what sort of financial shape you're in. Okay?"

"Then you should have costed the operation. Even with throwing in the paper at trade price, and fully automatic printing and folding and franking, the cost of 400,000 copies in the mail — even allowing for the new fax mail rates — is going to be . . . is going to be . . ." My voice faded to an undignified croak as I doodled some figures on my blotter.

"I can let you have eight thou in cash to prove I'm on the level, but that cleans me out. You'll have to rack up enough credit to cover the rest of your investment. You can do that, can't you?"

"Yes, but I don't like it."

"It's only for a couple of weeks, then you can cream it back off the top — before you pick up your third of a million or more. What more do you want?"

"A drink," I said firmly, producing a bottle of Tucker's Choice from the bottom drawer of my desk. Wynter nodded when I offered him a glass and we sat for another hour sipping bourbon and discussing practical details of the scheme and going over the letters he had already drafted. Sometime during that hour — partly because of the booze, partly because I was desperate for money, but mainly because I was impressed by the thoroughness of Wynter's pre-planning — I became totally committed to the adventure in applied mathematics.

After all, I told myself, even if it doesn't work out exactly as planned, we're bound to get some money back. It won't be the end of the world.

Hah!

It was almost eleven when I went into Trev's office and found he was still sitting in his thought projector. He is a very large young man, one of those poeple who insist on wearing T-shirts and tight jeans on figures which ought to be decently swathed. His face is huge, round and placid, un-marked by earthly cares, covered with the kind of fine golden fuzz that girls shave off their legs. His blue eyes look humorous when there is nothing to laugh at, and gravely concerned when there is nothing to worry about.

"Trev, what are you doing in here at this time?" I said, trying to control my annoyance.

"Having my mid-morning break," he replied, twinkling.

"How can you have a break before you've even started?" I pointed in the direction of the shop. "There isn't a single machine running out there."

His eyes clouded with sorrow, and for a moment I thought I had stirred his conscience. I should have known better.

"Aw, Des, don't tell me you've been at the liquor already." He heaved himself up out of his foil-lined box, a laborious operation which had to be carried out in stages. "Have you any idea what that stuff does to your body?"

"As long as it doesn't get like yours . . ."

"Unkind, Des," he said, but azure gleams showed he was unaffected by the insult. He picked up and swigged from a bottle of his favorite drink, a revolting locally-produced concoction known as Blissfizz, which was pink, opaque and loaded with sugar. It reminded me of calamine lotion, but Trev had been addicted to it since childhood and drank nothing else — a habit which no doubt had a lot to do with his excessive girth.

I decided to try sarcasm. "What's the good word from Betelgeuse? Have they given you clearance to do some work today, or are you going to be tied up with more important things?"

"I wish you wouldn't talk that way, Des." He fixed me with a worried stare. "The emissaries from the Kingdom of Orion are going to land real soon now and put their true believers in charge of the world. I'll probably be in control of the whole continent of North America, but even I won't be able to save you if you go around scoffing like that.''

"I'll take my chances.''

Trev extended three fingers of his right hand and made a priestly gesture. "May the Supreme Nizam forgive you, Des. I think maybe I ought to intercede with him . . .''

He made as if to climb back into his box, but I grabbed him and pushed his pudgy bulk into a chair. "Not now," I said, deciding to steer the conversation on to more constructive lines. "I've got some important work here. Charity work.''

"You?" Trev took a generous slug of Blissfizz and gave me a look which seemed almost worldly. "Charity work?"

"I'm a very charitable person, Trev, but lack of money has always prevented me from helping people the way I wanted to.''

"You'd have plenty of money if you didn't blow so much on rotgut whisky and fast cars and painted women,'' Trev accused. "There'll be none of that sort of thing when I'm in control.''

Only the need to be diplomatic prevented me from planting one on his downy chin. During our discussions Ralph Wynter and I had foreseen that some people on the sucker list would make a few discreet enquiries before entrusting us with their cash. For that reason our letters had to be signed by a real person, one with an unblemished record and whose name could be looked up in various directories. Trev was listed as company vice-president, had never been in any kind of trouble and nobody from out of town would have any reason to suspect he was a fully-fledged lollipop farmer — all of which made him ideal for our purpose. Wynter had been dubious before learning that Trev was so naive that he signed all the tax returns I prepared for him without ever reading what they said. He had left it to me to enlist Trev's aid without giving him any real idea of what we were doing.

"I want to atone for all my past sins," I said, laying on as much sincerity as I could. "I've thought of a great way of helping thousands of needy people — but I can't do it without your help."

Trev shook his head. "I don't know, Des. I'm pretty tied up with my meditation programme and the UFO observations and the meetings of the Orion Society."

"This won't take up any of your free time, and . . ." I paused as I got a sudden inspiration. "It would be a way of proving to me that you really do get thought messages from Betelgeuse. I might become a convert."

"Hey! That would be great, Des." A faraway look appeared in his eyes. "If you learned to play the harp I could make you one of the praise leaders in my Grand Temple."

"We can talk about all that after I've shown myself to be worthy," I said quickly, bringing out an advance list of the runners in the second race at Hillston, a meeting due to be held in three days' time, and set it in his lap. "Have a look at that."

He studied the sheet briefly then handed it back to me, his moon-like face registering intense disapproval. "You know what I think about gambling, Des. It's evil.''

"I know that *gambling* is evil, but what I'm proposing has nothing to do with gambling." I got closer to him by pulling up an empty Blissfizz crate and straddling it. "Listen, Trev, with the superhuman psychic powers you get from the Supreme Nizam you could easily predict which of these four horses is going to win, couldn't you? There'd be no element of chance involved.''

He pulled back from me, affronted. "You really do think I'm simple, don't you, Des? You think I'm a moron.''

"What do you mean?''

"Trying to get me to prostitute my divine gifts so that you can make money on the horses.''

"You've got it all wrong," I said, relieved by the confirmation that he really was simple. "I swear to you that I wouldn't place a single penny on a horse. I've never suffered from the gambling fever, but others aren't so fortunate. I've got a list of thousands upon thousands of poor wretches whose lives have been ruined because they fell into the clutches of the bookmakers. They're destitute, Trev — but you can help them. You can be their salvation.''

"How?''

"Don't you see? If we tip them the names of a few certain winners they can get their money back from the bloodsuckers. Can't you see the beauty and the rightness of it? We can turn the bookmakers' own weapons against them — make the punishment fit the crime. We might even put some of them out of business.''

"I like it," Trev mused, a messianic glitter appearing in his blue orbs. "And you promise you won't take personal advantage of my predictions?''

"Cross my heart!" I gave the list of runners back to him. "Do your stuff, Trev. Help me fight a holy war against the syndicates."

"I'll do it. And do you know what, Des? Next time I communicate with Betelgeuse I'm going to give you the full credit for coming up with this idea."

"Virtue is its own reward," I said modestly. "Now, what about this horse?"

He frowned at the list for a full minute, took a thoughtful pull at his bottle of Blissfizz, then shook his head and heaved himself to his feet. My fears that he was going to confess failure were dispelled when he opened a cupboard and took out an instrument I recognised as his UFO detector. This was a small telescope from which he had removed the object lens and in its place had jammed an old-fashioned radio tube. I had looked into it once out of curiosity and had seen nothing but an oily blur of light which split into concentric rings when I moved the telescope's sections — a phenomenon which apparently was enough to convince Trev that he was peering into other planes of existence. He put the UFO detector to his eye, moved the other end of the instrument up and down my list a couple of times and gave a satisfied grunt.

"That's it," he stated confidently. "Number four. Realrock Isle."

"Wonderful! We're in business." I brought Trev into my office and brandished in front of him the introductory letter from INSIDE INFORMATION INC., which was the name Wynter had

dreamed up for our phoney tipster organisation.
As I had expected, Trev did not even bother to
scan the lines of print. His aversion to reading
had in the past led to some monumental goof-offs
in the mailing service, but now it was proving
useful. He was standing there with a look of
dreamy fulfillment all over his peach-fuzzed
countenance when I handed him a pen.

He stared down at it. "What's this for?"

"I want you to sign the letter, Trev. It's only
right that you should get all the credit. You and
the Supreme Nizam."

"I'm beginning to think I misjudged you," he
said, taking the pen. "What about putting in the
name of the horse?"

"Don't worry — I'll strip that in at the bottom
before we go to press."

Trev nodded, satisfied, poked his tongue out
of the corner of his mouth the way he always did
when he was writing, and signed his name with
a flourish. *Trevor Q Botley*. I whisked the letter
away from under his hand, led him to the door
and told him he was free to return to his thought
projector if he wanted to bring Betelgeuse up to
date on all that had been happening. Unbeliev-
ably, he shook his head.

"I'd rather get to work," he announced. "This
is no time for sitting around. It's a time for action."

"Action?" A sense of unreality stole over me.
"Are you feeling all right?"

"This is important work, Des — not one of your
trivial money-grubbing commercial exercises. In
a project like this you'll find me zealous, industrious and untiring. You'll see."

Coming from anybody else those words would have been disquieting — I would have much preferred to carry out the mailing shot alone and unobserved — but in the case of Trev I was not unduly worried. When it comes to serious work he has an attention span of about three seconds and a lizard-like tendency to remain perfectly motionless for hours at a time. I led the way into the shop and got down to work immediately.

Up until around 1990 the reproducing of 400,000 copies of even a single-page letter would have been a task of considerable magnitude, but the advent of gamma ray multi-sheet printing changed all that. Simply by placing the master copy on a block of treated paper and giving it a short burst of non-divergent radiation I was able to print 5,000 good copies at a time. It took me fifteen minutes to prepare the first 100,000 copies of the letter, those bearing the name of the horse Trev had selected. I passed them over to him for feeding through the Mailomat IV, the lightning-fast robot which began printing each with a name and address from Wynter's list, folding, sealing, franking and stacking them in well-secured bundles.

True to form, Trev fell into a near-cataleptic trance in the middle of the operation. That gave me ample opportunity to peel the name of his horse off the master, strip in another one and print a further 100,000 copies. At that point Trev, apparently deciding he had had enough of being zealous, industrious and untiring, ambled off to his office to have his customary lunch of a quart of Blissfizz and a bag of nauseating confections known as Coco-blobs. It was a full hour before

he returned, and by then I had printed two more
100,000 lots with the names of the remaining
horses and was running them through the Mailomat.

He blinked with surprise as he glanced around
the shop and saw the stage the job had reached.
"Say, you've really been going some."

"A strange force seemed to be driving me on-
wards."

"I'm proud of you, Des," he said. "And I want
you to know you'll get your due reward for all
this work."

I gave him a suitably enigmatic smile.

There now had to be a three-day break in the
proceedings, time in which to let the letters reach
their destinations and be studied in 400,000
homes.

As there was nothing I could do until the chosen race at Hillston had been run, I worked hard
for the rest of the day on routine contracts and
that night — partly as a celebration, partly to re-
lieve nervous stress — blitzed a couple of my favourite clubs with all the vigour of Genghis Khan
and Attila the Hun rolled into one. Next morning
I woke up beside a sweet young thing called Kris-
tine, who demonstrated her essential good nature
by giving me a couple of Superseltzers and remaining silent while I dressed and tottered off
to work.

I got to the office shortly after eight and was
brewing coffee when, to my astonishment, Trev
opened the door and rolled in with a news sheet
tucked under his arm. He was wearing a dark
blue T-shirt on which he had painted the major

stars of Orion. As usual the constellation was somewhat lacking in grandeur because the central part of it was lost in the fold beneath his squabby breasts, but his round face was more animated than I had ever seen it.

"Boy, you sure look a mess," he said, inspecting me with a show of concern.

"Never mind how I look. What brought you in so early?"

Trev unfolded his paper. "I've been making my selection for today," he said importantly, "and it's Lightburn in the . . ."

"Hold it!" I snatched the paper from his grasp and dropped it into a waste bin. "There isn't going to be any selection today."

"But I thought we were going to rob the bookies to help the poor."

"We are, Trev, we are — but not every *day*! We've got to allow time for the poor to collect on the first bet so that they'll have money for the next one." Looking at Trev's perplexed expression I thought of a way to explain the dwindling scale of our charity work. "Besides, what we did yesterday cost me a lot of hard cash — I'll have to concentrate on some ordinary work for a while, then see how many more needy people we can help. The list probably won't be as big next time."

"Sorry, Des," he said, looking contrite. "I didn't realise the way it was."

"It's all right." I patted him on the shoulder and eased him out of the office. "Just you leave the boring old practical details to me. All you've got to do is come up with the winners when we need them. Okay?"

"You can count on me." He lumbered away

amid a creaking of floorboards, leaving me staring thoughtfully into the coffee percolator. One thing I had not anticipated was my cousin actually taking an interest in what was going on in the shop — even when running off leaflets for his own Orion Society he was wrapped up in daydreams so much that he would let any kind of mistake go by. On one lovely occasion he had issued a news sheet, typed up by a semi-literate temp, which had referred all the way through to the Kingdom of O'Ryan. To me it had looked better that way, more appropriate somehow, but apparently a few of the faithful were pretty annoyed about the blunder and had threatened to depose Trev.

Later in the day, when Ralph Wynter called in with a draft of the second message from INSIDE INFORMATION INC., I told him I was thinking of cutting Trev out of the operation and simply stripping in his signature on future letters. Surprisingly, he was against the idea.

"What we're doing isn't actually against the law," he said, staring meaningfully through his steel rims, "but there are large sums of money involved. Some people might get angry and there might be some embarrassing investigations and publicity. It might be advisable for us to take a long vacation."

"And leave Trev to face the music? I don't know if I could do that."

"Nobody's going to touch *him*. From what you told me, he's got the best defence in the world — his innocence. How could anybody even think of leaning on a simpleton who genuinely believed he was a holy crusader?"

I nodded, impressed by the slippery quality of Wynter's mind, and we went on to talk about more important things. Trev's behaviour continued to worry me though. Something about the project, as he understood it, seemed to have caught his imagination and his interest was still as high as ever when Monday — the day of the selected race — came round.

On several occasions when I went into his office I found him sitting in his thought box running his UFO detector up and down racing sheets, pausing only to munch a Coco-blob. Right up to the start of the race I was fretting about what I was going to say to him if, as was likely to happen, the 'wrong' horse came in first, and so it was with some trepidation that I called up the afternoon's sports pages on the Cathodata set in my office. I needn't have worried, however — Realrock Isle had walked it by ten lengths. A combination of relief and unexpected excitement sent me sprinting in to give Trev the news.

"Naturally Realrock Isle won," he said in a mild voice, arching his eyebrows at me. "What did you expect?"

Only then did I remember the rules of our game. "Of course, I knew it *had* to win if that's what the thought voices told you," I mumbled apologetically, doing my best to cover the slip. "It's just that when you're not used to this sort of thing it seems sort of . . . miraculous."

"You've so much to learn," he sighed, passing me a handful of racing sheets upon which one horse in every event had been underlined in red crayon. "Take your pick from the lot."

"Thanks, Trev." I flicked through the sheets

and was pleased to see that he had covered the race Wynter and I had selected for our next mailing — a five-horse affair the following Thursday at Argent Heights. This time the Supreme Nizam of Betelgeuse, speaking through the medium of a defunct thermionic valve shoved in the end of a Woolworth telescope, had decreed that a nag called Wheatgerm would be first past the post. I got Trev to sign the second letter and, leaving him to his meditations, went out to the shop and started to work.

This time I only had to deal with the 100,000 people from the original list who had been given the winner, and it was a comparatively easy job to split them into five lots of 20,000 and tip a separate horse to each lot. Just to be on the safe side in case Trev came out to do a little work, I put spare letters tipping Wheatgerm on top of each pile — making it look as though the entire mailing said the same thing — and only removed them as the piles were going into the Mailomat. The precaution proved unnecessary, because it was almost quitting time before Trev roused himself and by then all 100,000 letters had been loaded into the pneumotube and were well on their various ways.

I began to feel easier in my mind about how the operation was shaping up, and celebrated by going out on the town that night with an exotic young lovely who was a snake dancer at Lord Jake's Revue Bar. She ate enough to choke one of her pet pythons, but I had no qualms about the expense — I could feel it in my bones that all my troubles, financial and otherwise, would soon be a thing of the past.

The first faint intimation that my skeleton is a lousy fortune teller came on Thursday afternoon when Wheatgerm romped home so far ahead of the rest of the field that he was nearly placed in the previous race.

Judging by the odds he came in at the bookmakers were as surprised as I was, so I did a slightly peculiar and uncharacteristic thing. I knew that Trev had no cosmic forces working for him, and that it isn't really remarkable for somebody to pick two winners in a row, and yet I was unable to resist digging out the handful of racing sheets he had marked and comparing them with the Cathodata results. The way it worked out, he had chosen some thirty horses and out of that number precisely three, including Wheatgerm, had been winners.

To me that figure seemed about average for somebody making blind stabs with a pin, or even with an old radio tube, so I damped down the sparks of the crazy idea that had begun to glimmer at the back of my mind and began to think about the next phase of the project. We were down to 20,000 people who had been given two winners and now the mechanical side of the operation was becoming child's play. Trev made things easier by spending more and more time in his thought projector while he pored over racing sheets, and once again I didn't even have to ask him to pick a horse in our next four-horse race. He had chosen an animal called Prismatic and as it was the odds-on favourite I wasn't too surprised when it won fairly comfortably. Trev received the news with a calm shrug and handed me another bunch of marked-up sheets, including one on which he had underlined a horse called Foreign Exchange in our next four-horse race.

Pleased with the way we had settled into an undemanding routine, I split the remaining list of 5,000 clients into four equal lots, tipped each lot a different horse and had the whole mailing completed in less than half an hour. Past experience had taught me to be extra careful when everything in the garden seems lovely, but I was so bemused by the nearness of the first pay-off that I let myself be lulled into that famous false sense of security, and was totally unprepared for trouble when it came.

I had spent an entire evening at my apartment with Ralph Wynter, splitting a bottle of Tucker's Choice and perfecting the text of the letter we were going to send to our reduced roll of 1,250 lucky people who — when the fourth race was run — would have received advice of four straight winners. Even though I say so myself it was a masterpiece of psychological manipulation, one which played on their quasi-religious hopes so accurately that they were bound to fall over themselves in their rush to mail us their money. With the serious business completed, Ralph had called up a couple of well-endowed working girls he was friendly with, and we had spent a few hours sampling what a more poetic person might have called the garden of earthly delights.

I think I was still wearing a self-satisfied smile when I got into the office next morning and began to tidy up some routine business matters. Hard work is a good way to pass the time. The race we were interested in was at noon, and within seconds of its completion the result was flashed up on my Cathodata screen. A horse called Lamplighter had won by two lengths. Trev's selection, Foreign Exchange, had come in last, but all that did was prove that his previous record of success had been what I always knew it to be —pure dumb luck. Whistling cheerfully, I isolated the list of 1,250 people who had been tipped Lamplighter and went into the shop to send them the offers they wouldn't be able to refuse. Visions of a promised land of dollar green pastures were shimmering before my eyes.

So intent was I on the good work that I almost keeled over with shock when, a few minutes later, a crash of breaking glass followed by a tremulous and unearthly moan drowned out the faint whir of the machinery.

I spun round, dry-mouthed, and saw Trev standing in the doorway of my office. To be more precise, his great bulbous form was slumped against the jamb and one hand was pressed to the narrow margin between his eyebrows and hairline that he regards as a forehead. His face was pale as he lurched away from the door and crunched towards me through the fragments of the Blissfizz bottle he had dropped. I backed off from him, fearful that his mind had finally snapped.

"It's all over, Des," he said in a hollow voice. "I'm undone. The Supreme Nizam has abandoned me."

"He'd never do a thing like that," I soothed, wondering what in hell had happened. "Not to you."

He rolled his eyes, horribly. "I must have transgressed, Des. That's the only explanation."

I was still trying to figure out what explained what when my gaze was drawn to a point behind Trev, to the electronic glow emanating from my office which told me I had forgotten to switch off the Cathodata set. That explained everything. It was obvious that Trev had wandered in there and somehow had concentrated on the screen long enough to discover his prediction for that day's race had been wrong — and, to say the least of it, he was reacting badly. He was swaying around like a balloon man anchored only by his shoes and there was a real danger of some of my best equipment being toppled and damaged. Cursing my carelessness, I fought to steady him up, but it was like trying to wrestle a zeppelin full of water.

"I'm unworthy, Des," he groaned. "I'm going to be cast into the outer darkness. Woe is me."

Staggering around under each surge of his weight, I strove desperately for some way out of the jam and almost sobbed with relief when inspiration came. "Why are you saying these things, Trev? Would the Supreme Nizam keep giving you winners if he thought you were unworthy?"

He steadied up slightly. "But I got it wrong. I saw it on the screen."

"Saw what?" I queried. "Lamplighter came in first — just like you predicted."

"Huh?" A flicker of hope appeared in his eyes. "I . . . I was nearly sure I marked a different horse. Foreign something or other."

"Perhaps that's what you meant to do, Trev, but you're forgetting that Another was guiding your hand." I groped around in the inside pocket of my jacket, carefully counting sample letters from the last mailing, and whipped out one I knew to bear Lamplighter's name. "I mean, it's down here in black and white. You can't argue with that, can you?"

"You're right," he whispered, a look of joy appearing his eyes. He let go of me and hurried away, but not before I saw that he was on the verge of tears.

I felt a twinge of guilt over having conned him and made up my mind to give him a bonus, maybe fifty or a hundred bucks, when the big money came in. The first thing I did, however, was to search out and destroy all the racing sheets he had marked, then I unplugged the Cathodata and removed its fuse to forestall any further trouble. After that I completed the mailing and, having made sure that Trev wasn't within earshot, telephoned Wynter to let him know that the gravy train was about to arrive.

Actually, I saw very little of Trev during the next few days — he seemed to have taken up permanent residence in his thought projector — and that was just as well because the flood of mail which began to arrive was, of course, addressed to him. And it's no exaggeration to describe it as a flood!

I have to confess that right up to the moment it happened I didn't really believe the scheme would pay off according to plan. Deep down inside me there had lingered a fragment of scepticism which sneered that it was all too good to be true — but I was wrong. The loot came winging from all over the continent. Well over 200,000 dollars arrived in the space of three days, all of it in the form of cash or open postal drafts as we had specified in the letter. Among the bills there was a surprising number of sincere little thank-you notes from people who were moved by Trev's apparent philanthropy, but when we had separated those out and burned them Wynter and I were left with great heaps of beautiful, glorious, untraceable money. We felt like lying down and rolling in it.

After a hectic bout of celebrations we sent the usual spread of tips on a five-horse race to almost 1,250 paid-up clients, and I took a little time off to buy a new car and restock my wardrobe with the classiest gear I could find. When the race had been run we then had close on 250 people who were convinced that their benefactor — Trevor Q Botley — was the greatest thing since silent cornflakes, and to them was sent the letter which revealed that the syndicate bosses were turning nasty and that in view of the huge risks involved the only way INSIDE INFORMATION INC. could stay in business was by upping the ante to two grand a throw. To the thousand disappointed clients who had been tipped the losing horses we sent an entirely different letter which apologised for the mistake, hinting that powerful enemies had been the cause, and offering the next guaranteed winner for a mere hundred dollars.

Once again I began to experience sneaking doubts — after all, two thousand dollars is a lot of money — but I needn't have worried. Nearly half-a-million promptly arrived in registered envelopes, most of which also contained embarrassingly fervent letters of gratitude. Even Ralph Wynter was surprised by the response we got to the auxiliary missive. It seemed that many of our clients were quite prepared to forgive Trev for one little slip, and to prove it they coughed up to the tune of an extra 70,000 bucks. For days as we went through the lucrative final phase of the operation I wandered around in a dreamy euphoria, giggling aloud every now and then, and trying to understand why I had ever bothered to work when making real money was so ridiculously easy.

During that period Trev went on signing letters without reading them, and making predictions about horse races without even bothering to check the results. Apparently his traumatic moment of doubt and subsequent renewal of belief had attuned him more closely than ever to his ethereal friends in the residential section of Betelgeuse. It made him less aware of what was going on in real life. I was glad about that because his success rate continued to be abysmal and it would have been awkward for us had he found out what a rotten prophet he actually was.

The daily ritual of sorting the mail and dividing the spoils meant that Wynter was now spending quite a bit of time in the office, and inevitably there came the point at which I had to introduce him to Trev. My cousin put on a performance which under other circumstances would have embarrassed me to death.

"Forsake your worldly ways," he said to Wynter, ignoring his outstretched hand. "The emissaries from the Kingdom of Orion are coming. They'll be here soon."

"Is that a fact?" Wynter winked at me. "How soon?"

"Real soon." Trev spoke with priestly assurance. "The Supreme Nizam of Betelgeuse has decreed it."

"Yes, but *how* soon?"

Trev stared upwards for a moment, apparently seeking guidance from a light fixture in the ceiling. "Ten o'clock Thursday morning."

"That's nice," Wynter chuckled. "He'll be just in time for coffee."

Trev gave him a look of mingled disdain and pity, turned on his heel and strode out of the office. He slammed the door so hard the pressure wave almost made my ears pop.

"You were right about that guy," Wynter said, sticking his tongue out of the corner of his mouth and making an idiot face. Perhaps I had some remnant of family feeling for Trev, but Wynter's remark and the way he delivered it annoyed me. Also there had been a strange glint in Trev's baby blue eyes, a hint of intensity I had never seen before which made me wonder what was going on inside his head.

"You shouldn't have pinned him down to an exact time like that," I said. "I don't like the idea of popping his bubble."

Wynter shrugged carelessly. "Relax, Desmond. Nobody can pop that kind of bubble."

For some reason I couldn't quite put my finger on the comment gave me a chilly feeling, as though somebody had opened a door nearby and admitted a coiling snake of cold air.

By the time we got near the final greatly reduced stakes, Wynter and I had settled into a routine. Every morning about nine we picked up the mail, took it into my office, locked the door and began the pleasurable task of opening the envelopes and sorting and dividing the money. Had we used the simplified scheme there would have been very little mail to deal with at that stage, but Wynter's idea for 'reviving' clients who had been given only one loser was still yielding fair returns, and Thursday morning produced sizable stacks of money, postal drafts and letters of worshipful gratitude.

"This is okay, but I'm packing it in tomorrow," Wynter announced, polishing his steel rims with a tissue. "It's vacation time and I can feel Rio calling. You should pull out as well."

"Expecting trouble?"

He tapped a pile of letters. "Some of the people who went down are a bit churned up about it, but I don't think they're a real threat. The ones I'm worried about are the characters who want to come round here and kiss your cousin's feet. They could descend on us at any time — and that's something I hadn't planned for."

"I see what you mean," I said. "Perhaps I ought to . . ."

I never got round to finishing the sentence because at that moment I became aware of something very odd that was taking place right before my eyes. My desk faces the door of the office, only a few paces from it, and from where I sat I could see with perfect crystal clarity that the aluminum shootbolt was sliding back — all by itself! I had fitted that bolt personally and knew there was no way of moving it from the far side of the door, so the sight of it quietly slipping back through its guides did peculiar things to my stomach. Wynter noticed the startled expression on my face, but before I could say anything to him the door was flung open and Trev came striding into the room. He was wearing his best Orion T-shirt, the one on which he had sewed the gold epaulettes, and was brandishing his UFO detector.

"The appointed hour is nigh," he boomed. "It's almost ten o'clock, and time for you to repent and . . . and . . ." His voice faltered as his gaze was drawn towards the desk and took in the heaps of envelopes, letters and money.

"Why didn't you lock the door?" Wynter said accusingly.

"I *did*," I whispered, but there was no time to explain about the self-propelled bolt for Trev was advancing on me with anger and reproach in his eyes. He looked bigger than ever, oddly majestic.

"Des, Des," he said, eyes burning me like blue lasers, "why have you committed this terrible sin? You gave me your word."

"This isn't what it looks like," I replied hurriedly, trying to calm him down. "Ralph and I have started this little mail order business. It's nothing to do with the horses. We sell . . . we sell . . ."

"Bibles," Wynter put in.

I nodded emphatically. "Bibles."

A story like that would have satisfied the old familiar Trev, but this new and rather disquieting one snatched up a handful of letters and subjected them to intense scrutiny. "You're lying to me, Des," he said. "You've been lying to me all along. These people believe in me, and you've been taking money from them. I'm disappointed in you."

"I've had enough of this crap." Wynter stood

up and motioned for me to do the same. "Let's throw the clown out of here."

"Good idea," I said, suddenly realising how dumb I had been to let somebody like Trev knock me off balance. Wynter and I were closing in on him when the second very strange thing occurred.

"Do not move," Trev commanded, raising his UFO detector as though it were some kind of talisman, and on the instant of his speaking I was gripped by a sudden and complete paralysis. Unable to believe what was taking place, I frantically willed myself to move forward and nothing happened — I was frozen into the immobility of a statue. Wynter was similarly petrified, locked in mid-stride, and judging by the expression on his face he was very unhappy about it.

For a moment Trev seemed almost as surprised as we were. His gaze shuttled between our faces and the UFO detector a few times, and I saw a look of wondering surmise appear in his eyes. He raised the detector again and, with his lips working silently, pointed it at one of my filing cabinets. The cabinet immediately turned into a stack of Blissfizz crates.

"It has happened," Trev breathed. "It's all coming to pass. The Supreme Nizam is rewarding the faithful." A faint halo sprang into being around his head as he waved the modified telescope again and turned the money on my desk into a small heap of withered leaves. Wynter gave a strangled moan.

At that point the evidence in favour of Trev's weird theories about the Kingdom of Orion was becoming pretty convincing, but in spite of every-

thing I still couldn't accept them. Fantastic
things, miraculous things, were happening all
round me — but there had to be a better explanation than that the Supreme Nizam of Betelgeuse was dropping in to visit my simple-minded
cousin. I sometimes get flashes of intuition, and
at that moment my mind suddenly seized on the
last word Trev had uttered — faithful. Faith,
somebody once said, can move mountains. Trev
had always had faith, lots of it, but not enough
to make any difference to anything in the material
world, so the inference was that he had obtained
reinforcements. And I — God help me — had
been instrumental in bringing up those reinforcements.

Thanks to my trickery and manipulation of
him, Trev was genuinely convinced he could
predict the future, and furthermore there were
many people throughout the country who also
believed in him because they had had incontro-
vertible 'proof' of his powers. Wynter had stressed
the religious element in the make-up of the compulsive gambler, and indeed we had relied on it
to make the scheme work. I have never been myst-
ically inclined, but in the moment of stress I
could see clearly that the faith and fervour of our
remaining clients was forming a reservoir of
psychic power which Trev could tap at will. He
had become a miracle-worker. In a way it was
almost surprising that his transformation had not
occurred at an earlier stage in the game, but perhaps the mental force of 5,000 people who are
fairly well convinced of something is less than
that of fifty who are total believers.

The insight I had received was a terrifying one,

but it provided some sort of explanation for what was going on — and it also showed me a possible way out of the situation. They key factor was Trev's own faith in his powers, and if I had built that faith up I should also be able to tear it down and restore him to his former state of ineffectual goofiness.

"I have a confession to make," I said to Trev, relieved to find he had left me the power of speech. "Ralph and I *have* been making money out of this thing with the horses. We've been duping people all along. It was what we set out to do, right from the beginning."

Trev eyed me with sorrow. "You're a broken reed, Des."

I nodded. "The point is, Trev, that we even duped you. Nearly all the predictions you made about the races were wrong. I fooled you into thinking you were getting them right."

"That doesn't make sense," he said, giving me a calm and pitying smile. "You showed me the letters yourself. And why are the people I helped still sending you their money?"

"But those are only a fraction of the number we started out with."

"That's right," Wynter chimed in, apparently sensing what I was trying to do. "You see, my whole plan was based on starting off with a huge . . ."

"Silence!" There was a look of Mosaic anger on Trev's round face as he turned on Wynter. "You are the one who corrupted by cousin, you are the serpent — and you shall be punished accordingly."

He raised his UFO detector, waved it once —

and Wynter disappeared. For a second I thought he had simply been dematerialised, then I saw there was a tiny speckled snake wriggling on the floor right where he had been standing. I stared down at it in dismay. Trev, revealing a ruthless streak I didn't even know he possessed, completed Wynter's punishment by raising one of his boots and stamping hard on the snake, converting it into a revolting mess.

"My God," I quavered. "This is terrible."

"You have nothing to fear from me," Trev said. "You are a weak man, Des, prey to all the desires of the flesh, but you have a hidden core of goodness. I have forgiven you for your sins and will give you a place by my side as soon as . . . Well, as soon as . . ." His words tailed away uncertainly.

I had been staring at him for several nervous seconds before it dawned on me that he had no idea what to do next, that he was all dressed up with supernatural powers and epaulettes on his T-shirt, and had nowhere to go. My gaze followed his to the clock on the office wall. The time was ten after ten, which meant that the Supreme Nizam was late for his appointment. Trev gnawed his lower lip and I could see he was having difficulty in reconciling himself with the notion that a Lord of Orion could have human faults such as tardiness.

"How about that?" I said, seizing the chance. "It's way after ten and there hasn't been any cosmic visitation. Can't you see what this means, Trev? It proves . . ."

"Clam up," Trev said irritably and, having seen

what he could do to people who displeased him,
I clammed up. He brooded for a moment, his face
looking more and more like that of the Trev I
knew, and I began to hope against hope that the
bubble of his beliefs had been punctured. I studied his halo, trying to decide if it had shrunk or
grown dimmer. It may have been my imagination
at work, but it seemed to me that his aura really
was on the wane.

I was beginning to feel quite optimistic about
my chances of escaping from him when he got
one of his inspirations. He raised the UFO detector to his eye and aimed it at the ceiling. There
was a moment of silence and then, to my consternation, a look of inhuman elation spread over
his chubby features. He snapped the telescope
shut, almost dislodging the radio tube from the
end of it, and turned to me.

"I've been a fool," he said, beaming. "I don't
know what came over me, Des. All that stuff
about the Supreme Nizam coming here — it was
pure nonsense."

"Don't worry about it," I soothed, hardly able
to credit my luck. "Anybody can make a little
mistake."

Trev shook his head. "It wasn't a little mistake,
Des — I got the message completely wrong. You
see, the Supreme Nizam wants me to go to *him!*"

"Hold on a minute," I said, my voice rising
into a bleat of alarm as new vistas of peril opened
up in my mind.

"I don't have a minute." Trev raised his arms
and now he really was huge and awesome. "My
work on Earth has ended. The time has come for

me to lead the faithful to the Kingdom of Orion."

I made an attempt to pull his arms down again, but I was too late.

The floor gave a sickening lurch, the office walls dissolved and blew away like mist, and all at once I was standing with Trev at the centre of a circular landscape about the size of a football field. It was a surrealistic landscape, dotted with ornate fountains and artificial-looking trees covered with small tufts of white. Beyond the perimeter was a hard blackness, and when I turned to my left I could see the blue-white disk of the Earth floating on a background of stars. I moaned aloud as it came to me that I was out in space and travelling through the interplanetary void in a kind of environmental bubble conjured up by Trev. I fell on my knees before him and tugged at the hem of his T-shirt.

"Have mercy on me," I pleaded. "I don't want to go to Betelgeuse — please send me back to Earth."

"Can't do that," he said in voice full of compassion. "Earth is no more."

He made a casual gesture with his UFO detector as he spoke, and the Earth winked out of existence.

I cringed away from him. "Wha . . . what have you done, Trev? All those people . . ."

"Not all of them." He gave me one of his terrifying indulgent smiles. "The harvest of the faithful is safely gathered."

At that moment I became aware that there were about fifty people wandering around the circumscribed Dali landscape, their faces blanked out with shock. I recognised several as members of Trev's Orion Society, and could only surmise that the rest were 'all-winner' clients of INSIDE IN-FORMATION INC. The whole affair must have been even more traumatic for them than it had been for me, but I didn't get time to sympathise with their plight.

Trev waved his telescope and suddenly all of us were dressed in unisex garments which took the form of ankle-length robes. I looked down at the unfamiliar object which had materialised in my hands and saw that it was a small harp.

"Come, my children," Trev called in a voice of thunder. "Come and sing the praises of the Supreme Nizam of Betelgeuse, who has called us to our rightful places in the Kingdom of Orion. The journey will take many years, but do not worry — there is an abundance of food and drink. Now, sing!"

Raising our voices in unison — because there is no way to disobey Trev's commands — and with me plinking dispiritedly on the harp, we began to sing.

That was three years ago and we've been trav-elling through space ever since. I've become as fat as a hippo through lack of exercise and having to get all my nourishment from the Coco-blob trees and the Blissfizz fountains. With Trev in complete control of things here inside his space bubble life is, as you might imagine, hellishly boring — no booze, no decent food, no sex, and we spend sixteen hours a day singing the bloody awful hymns he composes.

I don't mind telling you, the only thing that keeps me from going mad is trying to figure out what is going to happen when we finally get to Betelgeuse.

JUST ANOTHER END OF THE WORLD
by
Maxim Jakubowski

When the acid rains fell, we were all in the convention's hospitality lounge, lazing about or playing pool. Whether the heavy rains were actually part of World War Three or just an ominous portent of darker things soon to follow, I do not know. They came in awful quietness in the small hours of the night, with little spectacular or melodramatic rolls of thunder or pyrotechnic lightning. Some girl remarked "Oh, it's raining outside!" but we attached no importance to this, stoned, tired or just gently drunk that we were all. In retrospect, maybe we should have begun worrying then; it was deepest summer and the weather had been splendidly consistent and hot for the last few weeks.

When the pieces fell out of the sky (literally), I was sitting in some dark corner chatting up an attractively nubile Swedish sub-editor with incredibly deep grey eyes, a complexion the colour of pale roses and a figure that had me gasping with delight long before I had even manoeuvred

myself towards laying a hand on her. Trout and
Jo Herovit were arguing loudly about some roy-
alties due on an anthology one of them had recently got back into print. Priest and Sheckley
kept on playing pool, handling their cues with
almost as much dexterity as their typewriters.
Brunner, as suave as ever, was practicing his
heavily-accented Albanian on a Yugoslav pub-
lisher, reminding him pointedly that there were
still a few of his early Ace double adventure novels that hadn't seen the light of day in Zagreb.
My blonde companion, Agnetha, looked up and
said:

"Zere are fings falling from ze sky." (which
sounded more French than Swedish but ours is
not to reason why).

"So they are," I said, not even looking in the
direction of the window. Nothing was going to
deflect me from my course of action. A rebuff the
night earlier from a woman who, on first being
approached by me "hello and who are you?", had
informed me with a joyous smile all over her face
that "oh, I'm just the wife of a rock musician and
I have a beautiful eighteen-month old baby" was
enough for one convention.

Then Colvin, deeply ensconced in an armchair
near the lounge windows, dozing in a cloud of
pot, appeared to wake up and screamed:

"Bloody hell, it's a fuckin' pandemonium out
there!"

And when the sky went fiery red, we all
stopped what we were doing and peered anx-
iously out of the windows and watched in silence
as the lights of the world went off. The sky shifted
like a mad laser show through a rainbow of col-
ours dug up from hell and elsewhere.

"I think this is *it*," some one said.

"Yeah, the very last Convention," added a joker.

I went for the phone. The line was dead.

"What did you expect?" Jake Ash asked me. "The power's gone. I think nobody should leave this lounge for the time being. Lock the door."

When the darkness came, harder than coal, blacker than the blackest night, I think we all sort of shivered, realising that some of our worst imaginings and dreams were actually becoming reality, and, this time around, we weren't going to be paid for them either . . .

A historic moment, I thought ironically, here comes World War Three and I am witnessing the end of science fiction, standing here hopeless, scared shitless in the midst of a science fiction convention. No doubt the fifty or sixty (fifty-eight, we later found out) writers and editors present were all thinking along similar lines.

Together with the darkness, came the silence, as we quickly realised the time for jokes was over. A heavy silence, redolent of eternity, just a cough here, some guy sniffing there or a woman trying to contain her tears.

I felt a hand in mine. Agnetha. She moved closer to me. My eyes were still locked onto the blank landscape of desolation beyond the closed windows of the hospitality suite. I felt the warmth of her body against mine, stirring my loins and other delicate parts of my anatomy.

"If this is how it's all going to end," a voice in the darkened room said, "I know how I want to go."

Some women sighed.

Agnetha's nails were already frantically

scratching my back, digging into my flesh with sheer desperation.

If it's radiation, I reflected, we've only a few hours left.

My mouth reached for hers, tongues establishing contact, a bridge, moist pleasurable feeling. Similar sounds filtered through to us from around the large room. At any rate, science fiction writers are realists, I mused, as we lowered ourselves to the floor in a frantic embrace.

It wasn't radiation. They'd probably used some new 'clean' weapons and bombs. But it was the end of the world. That is, the world as we used to know it.

In the morning, charcoal grey sky peering through the windows, surprised at all still being alive, we looked at each other shiftily, a bit red in the face, somewhat embarrassed by the sexual excesses of the previous night. We dressed and moved uneasily around in the room that now smelt disagreeably of rancid smoke, sweat and sundry other excretions.

"Well, I feel fine," said Mike Jones.

"So do I. No trace or feeling of sickness," said Sid Snot.

"What now?"

We talked a lot amongst ourselves, argued a great deal, trying to remain rational, but then decided unanimously that something should be done. We would open the door, at least explore the rest of the hotel and, later maybe, venture outside.

Those first few days after the catastrophe are not memories I wish to dwell upon at length, although, all these years later, I still often awake in the middle of the night, shivering, sweating profusely, heart of ice, heart of glass, remembering the desolation, the corpses, the smells, the decaying bodies, the dead children, the despair, the fear, the animals, the mass graves we had to dig, the sheer absurdity of it all. Why us? Why them?

But the most eerie thing was to cross the empty cities, littered with the rotting leftovers of civilisation, derelict but still somehow alive, shop windows still full of glittering goods, all now ours but somehow suddenly devoid of any real attraction.

Of course, with all our combined literary apocalyptic background, we should have known what to expect. After all, wasn't this just another end of the world. For days, we thought our time on earth wouldn't last much longer; that the loophole that had allowed our freak survival would tighten on us, that the reprieve was only temporary. Naturally, we came up with many theories, easy and abstruse, but whoever was right was of little importance, the only thing that now mattered was that, through some unknown fluke, we were now the only survivors. The hospitality lounge of the convention hotel had inexplicably been spared the horror of the great death.

In the outside world, the buildings still stood, generally unharmed, the factories, the fertile fields, but every other human being had succumbed. Instantly. At least, seemingly painlessly.

Having recognised there only seemed to be us, talk changed from past science fiction end of the worlds to our present predicament and we heartily began making plans. Some of us cycled (using abandoned cars was too problematic; the lack of electricity to man the pumps rendered further petrol supplies problematic) to the nearest cities to obtain confirmation of the global state of the catastrophe; tried radio stations. No other survivors were found. What had it been about the shelter of the convention hotel that had saved us? We never did find out, and the problem puzzles us still now.

"I remember writing a story just like this in the sixties," said Lawrie Marsh.

"Oh yeah?" remarked Sid Snot. "And what did your survivors do? Rebuild civilisation singlehanded?"

Marsh sort of blushed inside his bushy beard and answered:

"Yes. With many attendant problems, but they managed it. I was a bit disappointed when the story didn't get a nomination for the annual prizes."

So, we decided to rebuild civilisation.

Or, at any rate, a semblance of life.

Oddly enough, the feminist writers and editors in our midst (or should I say former writers and editors) were the most vehement when it came to the delicate problem of procreation, you know, the continuation of the species. The solution we arrived at was utterly logical, if a bit lacking in delicacy (I'd always been a bit of a sentimental bugger, even in my new wave speculative days). I wouldn't have minded one bit keeping sweet Agnetha's body all my own, but a controlled form

of promiscuity was decided on for the final good
of our human race, and so I obeyed the rules.
Close your eyes and think of mankind became an
occasional motto . . .

We left the city and chose a small country village within easy distance. Food would be no
problem for a long time; supplies of canned goods
were available in abundance in the stores of the
area and would last more than a lifetime and by
then, anyway, the crops planted and planned
would already be feeding the majority of our er-
satz colony. We discovered a generator in a barn
and two of the ex-engineers in our group of writers were soon made responsible for energy matters, thus keeping our discomforts to a minimum.
We were ready for it, but the lack of all the modern amenities we had previously been accus-
tomed to was something else again. Jobs and
functions were allocated as best we could, according to the talents we had, prior to our willing
slavery to the typewriter and the pen. We for-
tunately numbered three doctors, two nurses,
various technicians, a botanist who came in very
useful, Ike French the biochemist whose knowledge was absolutely encyclopedic, an astrophy-
sicist who was an expert at baking bread, a
psychologist who soon switched to psychiatry
and proved useful in soothing our frequent nightmares full of death and doom. A resourceful
group. Having spent four years in merchant bank-
ing before going freelance, quite some time back,
I was given the job of administering the logistics
of the settlement, Camp Tomorrow as we now
called it. Money didn't of course come into it, as
there was no longer any need for it, but you'd be

surprised at the paperwork involved in running everything smoothly, coordinating our varied but necessarily urgent activities.

The first winter hit us hard and we lost three, among the oldest. But, with spring, came the first births. Agnetha's was the second, by a few days only, and although there was no way of being certain, the baby had a familiar grin and dimple in his chin that played havoc with the strings of my heart. We called him Adam. A symbolic name, the first man and all that. The first baby born forty eight hours earlier had been a girl. Her name was Joanna (although the mother's name had been Eve . . .).

Work in the fields progressed satisfactorily and we soon began making our first steps towards self-sufficiency. Two elderly lady editors set up the nursery and heated discussion quickly sprang up, as to how we should educate the new children. Every single one of us had very definite ideas on the subject and, not surprisingly, our views all differed quite radically. Compromises were reached. At about the same time, our chemists succeeded in modifying several old cars and tractors to run on our own home-made fuel (made from waste material).

Night.

Watching the crimson sails of sunset gliding over the distant horizon of the mid-west plains, I couldn't help feeling perversely disappointed that things were working out for our ill-assorted group, it was just like another hack novel! Foiled again Satan! The world will not end.

Agnetha was pregnant again, as were eleven other women. This was going to be a permanent feature of our ladies for many years to come.

Adam was just about beginning to walk, stumbling joyful steps, twinkling eyes, healthy appetite, full of surplus energy. I closed my eyes, remembering the desolate landscape all the travelers to the ends of time in my stories of old had encountered. Images of emptiness and white chalky desolations, cliffs of marble running into the dead seas, a sky the colour of woe, silence eternal, sun fading fast out there in space, no longer bathing the planet with its flames of life. Of course, we now had the empty cities, full of dread and past horrors, but we seldom ventured there any longer. Most animals had also died in the catastrophe, so the buildings and metropolis streets were safe, but the urban architecture only served to remind us of the first days after: the bodies, the utter despair. So we purposefully avoided them. Just a foray for stocks of canned food, spare parts, equipment, reading matter or medicine every few months, in a safe group of at least twelve.

I opened my eyes. The sky was now darker, full of stars, every dot of light a beacon of hope for the future that lay ahead of us. I turned round. Agnetha was sleeping. Her round belly bulged through the bed cover, a look of peace on her face. I walked silently towards the bed, kissed her gently on her lips, brushing stray hair away from her eyes and joined her inside the bed. The wooden beams of the farmhouse creaked a little around us as the temperature outside grew colder. In the hearth, a small wood fire still shone red and warm.

Time. Healer of wounds.
Seasons going by, rhythm of the crops, of the

land, trees growing, plants and flowers born, dying, being born again. Cycles of life.

Years. Always so short, too short. One is gone already and another begins before you even realise.

The children have grown, sturdy as trees and the joyful noises from the school in the old Presbyterian church keep getting louder all the time (we don't require churches any longer). Soon, there will be enough children to occupy the village school; until now, it had proved too large and unpractical for its originally designated function.

Already, the first deaths from old age among our early contingent, Marsh, Steinberg, Korzeniowski, Orf, Frances Lengel, Luke Ilje, sedentary bodies grown prematurely old because of the constant toil, the sweat, the hidden grief. Discreet autumn burials, with no florid speeches or unnecessary sentimentality. Oh my, have we grown so hard and insensitive, that we can no longer shed a genuine tear of bitterness?

Today, Agnetha discovered her first white hairs. I just smiled; I'd had mine since my mid-twenties. Always thought they made me look distinguished . . .

Funny how time goes by.

Camp Tomorrow has become virtually self-sufficient with the coming of age of the second generation, while we original survivors gradually become redundant, useless, not strong enough any longer for the work in the fields or building the new block extending the old town-hall. Adam now has two small children of his own, and the "kids," as we all still call them, are becoming increasingly active in the Organisation Council Meetings, dealing with Camp strategy and the day-to-day running of things.

Yesterday, after the evening communal meal, some of us oldens got talking of old times, complaining of all the free time we now had and the ensuing boredom.

"I've finally read all Dostoievsky. What do I do now?"

"And I, Proust."

"Maybe we should all start writing again," I suggested, half in jest. "It's the only thing we used to do well, after all."

Jake Ash roared with laughter.

"Best idea I've heard in years," he said.

Most of the others agreed.

"I don't know if I could remember how again," remarked Frippeni, who had never been very prolific, constantly struggling with writer's block.

"But what's the point of us all writing again, if no one is going to read us?" some one said.

"Why shouldn't they?" I pointed out. "There's a printing press in the basement of the old local newspaper offices. We could spruce it up, get it working again."

I could feel shivers of excitement coursing through the smoked-up room. Their blood was once more pulsing in fourth gear.

"Paper?" Trout asked. "We won't find enough paper to print books by every one of us." Always a spoilsport, old Trout.

"Who's talking about whole books, novels," I said. "We're too rusty for that yet, anyway. Let's all start writing short stories again."

"Yes," said Agnetha. The editor in her was awakening, after all the years of motherhood and devotion to the cause. "I've always been a sucker for thematic anthologies . . ."

"But does it have to be science fiction?" I asked, having once seriously flirted with the mainstream.

"Yes!" they all shouted back in unison.

And we've chosen our first theme, all fired by a common enthusiasm. At last, having rebuilt civilisation, life now has a meaning for us old troopers of the imagination wars.

The theme was obvious. It didn't take us long to find it. Every one says he has absolutely great ideas. We've all sworn to outdo ourselves on this one.

So, here I sit, chuckling mischievously, writing my own downbeat end of the world story, writing my life away.

Ursula K. Le Guin

POUL ANDERSON